the Forgotten Ones

LAURA HOWARD

The Forgotten Ones
Book One of
The Danaan Trilogy

Copyright © 2013 by Laura Howard
Interior design by JT Formatting
Published by Finding Bliss Publishing

ISBN-13: 978-0615809052
ISBN-10: 0615809057

Find out more about the author and upcoming books online at **http://laurahoward78.blogspot.com/** or like her on Facebook at **https://www.facebook.com/LauraHoward78**

Dedication

*For Mom,
for never telling me I couldn't.
I miss you every minute.*

Chapter One

I caught a glimpse of my mother staring out the den window. She held her violin loosely under her chin, and the bow dangled from her fingertips. Her jaw was slack, her eyes locked on something in the trees beyond me. I knew that haunted expression. I froze.

I swallowed hard as her eyes shifted to me. The violin fell from her chin, and I could see her bottom lip trembling.

I should have been used to that reaction from her when she saw me during an episode. It happened every time. But I wasn't.

I flew into the house as fast as my feet would carry me. The screen door crashed behind me as I came to a halt outside the den. My mother clutched fistfuls of her blonde hair, garbled words spilling from her lips.

"I have to. I have to go out there," she said. "He's waiting for me."

She stood in the semi-darkness, mumbling, the only other sound the hum of the ceiling fan. I clung to the doorjamb as I watched my grandmother approach carefully.

She placed her hands on my mother's shoulders, and on contact my mother's body stopped quaking. Gram crooned, rocking her back and forth, as she pulled her into her arms and led her away from the window.

My stomach tightened, and I backed away to leave them alone. If she saw me again, who knew what would happen.

I cringed as the floor creaked beneath me, and she jerked her head in my direction. Her eyes widened when she saw me, and the shaking began again. Breaking away from my grandmother, she stumbled backward toward the window. She raked her fingers down her face and hair as she moaned. "Liam…" Tears streamed down her cheeks, causing thick strands of hair to stick to her face.

I entered the room slowly, desperate not to step on another squeaky floorboard. Her green eyes burned into mine, and I locked my eyes on hers. No matter how many times she fought my attempts to soothe her, I had to keep trying. She was my mom.

I reached for her shoulders. "Mom," I whispered. "It's just me."

She flinched. I knew she recognized me. I'd never met my father, but under my mattress I hid the only scrap I could find with his image on it. The picture—a strip of them actually—was taken before I was born in a photo booth in Ireland. I looked just like him. Considering how she often spoke his name when she was like this, my gut told me that she saw my father in me.

She writhed as I touched her and clawed at my hands. Gurgling sounds came from somewhere deep in her throat, but I knew she was still saying my father's name. I placed my hands gently over hers, my gaze steady, as though approaching a wounded animal. I took deep, soothing breaths the way Gram had taught me.

I could feel the weight of Gram's stare, watching as I got closer than ever to my mother actually letting me comfort her. I focused on my mom, ignoring the panic rising in my chest.

"Shh..you're okay," I said. "You're okay." I repeated it over and over, softly, until her breathing became even, more normal. It felt like hours, but the tension in her fingers loosened eventually as she stopped trying to resist me.

My grandmother walked out of the room as I continued to make shushing sounds, the panic in my mother's eyes fading. I couldn't see it, but I knew Gram was probably smiling, at least a little.

I exhaled and led my mother to the couch. The same woman who had just been in the throes of a schizophrenic episode was now completely unresponsive as she sat.

Out of the corner of my eye, I could see Gram standing just outside the doorway. I released my mother's hands—she'd stay that way for a while, and there was nothing any of us could do—and got up to follow Gram down the hallway to the kitchen. The air wafted toward me as she moved, smelling like oranges and cloves—familiar and comforting.

I opened the refrigerator, snagged a bottle of water, and slouched down at the kitchen table. I tried to smile as I unscrewed the cap, but inside I was struggling with the gratification of being able to bring my mother down from her episode versus the pang of guilt for being the one who caused her condition in the first place. Before I was born, she'd been a bright, happy college student. Her spiral into schizophrenia didn't start until I showed up.

She had met my father during her last year of college. She had traveled to Ireland for her final semester to study music at Trinity College in Dublin. She'd been fine when she left, I'm told, but when she came back she was heartbroken and pregnant. She'd never been the same since.

"Have you eaten, honey?" Gram asked, nailing me in place with her eyes.

I flipped the bottle cap in my fingers. "No, but I'm fine."

"Oh no, you don't. We had a nice steak for supper, cooked just the way you like. You'll have some, won't you?"

I had to laugh. With Gram there was no choice, even if she asked. I sat down at the table while she whirled around the kitchen. In minutes I had a steak dinner in front of me, complete with steaming mashed potatoes and green beans.

"You spoil me, you know," I said between bites. "I'm never going to be able to take care of myself if you keep this up."

Gram smiled at me. "You'll have plenty of time to take care of yourself. Let me spoil you while I still can."

I swallowed down the guilt, knowing she didn't see raising me—and Mom—for the past almost twenty-two years as the burden it felt like to me.

As I ate, my mother walked into the kitchen. She sat down at the table quietly without looking at either of us.

"Hi, Mom…" I spoke as softly as I could, not wanting to alarm her.

"Hello." Her voice was barely more than a whisper. She chewed on her fingernail and stared absently out the window. Even with the hair framing her face in knots, my mother looked lovely. Her eyes sage green, her skin flawless. She was forty-three but didn't look a day over thirty.

"That was a beautiful tune you played earlier, Beth," Gram said as she took my mother's hands in her own. "I could practically smell the breeze blowing in off the Irish sea."

"Mm hmm," my mother answered, mostly detached, but a tiny smile lifted the corner of her mouth.

My cell phone buzzed in my pocket, and I pulled it out quickly before it startled my mom. I opened it to find a message from my cousin, Nicole:

I need ice cream tonight

I gave a small laugh as I put my phone back into my pocket. I'd worked all afternoon at my grandfather's hardware store, but it was Friday night—I should've known I wouldn't be able to just relax with a good book. Nicole was twenty, only a year younger than me, and we were as close as sisters. But our ideas of a perfect Friday night couldn't be more different. If only we didn't live next door to each other maybe I could get out of this.

I glanced out the window to Nicole's driveway. When I'd gotten home, it had been filled with cars—her friends had been taking over the place. But now I was grateful to only see her little Jetta. Hanging out with Nicole I guess I could handle.

Her friends were a different story. Especially when Ethan Magliaro was around.

Chapter Two

Nicole and I sat down at a table on the patio with two of the biggest sundaes on the menu at DeeDee's. The sun was hanging low in the evening sky, and the heat from earlier in the day had settled into pleasant warmth on my skin. The last fingers of golden light caused the pink and blue umbrellas to cast a glow across Nicole's pale blonde hair. She licked a puff of whipped cream off her spoon and eyed me.

"What?" I said through a mouthful of ice cream.

"We're going to the beach tomorrow," she said before taking her own bite.

"Have fun," I mumbled.

She wiped her lips with a napkin and narrowed her eyes at me. "You're coming." I opened my mouth to argue, but she held a slender finger up at me and pursed her lips. "It's the first Saturday you've had off in months. School's over, at least for the summer. You're coming."

I sighed and looked up at the pattern of our umbrella. "You really know how to ruin a perfectly good sundae."

Her eyes shot daggers at me. "We'll have a great time, Al." Her expression changed as she seemed to change tactics. Her green eyes widened and her lip stuck out just the tiniest bit.

Cranky Nicole was a challenge, but pouting Nicole was impossible.

"Fine," I sighed. "We're going to the beach." I looked at my sundae, which had made me so happy a minute earlier and a thought came to me. She hadn't said anyone else was coming, but Nicole and her boyfriend Jeff were practically inseparable. "Wait, who else is going?"

Nicole grinned, clearly smelling her victory. "The usual crew: Jeff, Rachel, Sean and"—her eyebrows inched up—"Ethan."

I nodded, trying to breathe evenly. I hated the way my pulse spiked at just the mention of his name. Handsome, cocky Ethan. His smile had the power to break down every one of my defenses. But, I didn't have space in my life for that. I had a plan—to focus on taking care of my mom. My grandparents had done it by themselves for long enough. I needed to find a way to help, to unburden them. That was my priority. But Ethan…he was so hard to resist sometimes.

Just as I began to get lost in thought, a quick movement caught my eye as Jeff snuck up behind Nicole. He held his finger to his lips and planted a kiss on Nicole's cheek.

She jumped and instinctively smacked him, but a smile overtook her face when she realized who it was.

"Hey, babe." Jeff took the seat next to her and looked over at me. "Hey, Al."

The chair next to mine scraped the patio, and it was my turn to jump. Ethan dropped into the seat and grinned at me, his dimples out in full force. I tried to concentrate on my sundae.

"Hey," he said, nodding at me. A brown curl slipped down his forehead, adding to his annoying charm.

"Hi," I muttered before shoving a glob of half-melted ice cream in my mouth to avoid conversation. *Must. Not. Fall.* I reminded myself.

Ethan was tall, olive-skinned with dark, messy curls. Easily the best-looking guy in Stoneville. And also the biggest player in town. He knew the effect he had on girls, and he used it to his advantage.

"So, we're all set for the beach tomorrow," Nicole told them. She sounded a little too smug, and I rolled my eyes.

"Something in your eye, Allison?" Ethan asked, seemingly amused at my attempt at indifference.

I clenched my jaw and almost rolled my eyes again. "That must be it, Ethan."

"Oh, come on. I know how bad you want to see me with my shirt off."

I knew it didn't warrant a response, but I could never keep my mouth shut when Ethan provoked me. And he knew it.

"The entire female population of this town has seen you without a shirt on. *Not* that exciting."

A slow smile spread across his face—he saw through me. I really needed to work on my sarcasm.

He turned back to Nicole and Jeff, who were debating whether to head northeast to Hampton Beach or southeast to Horseneck Beach the next day. Not a debate I had any interest in. Though, maybe it could be okay…it was a day off after all.

Nicole's petite nose scrunched up. "Hampton is full of screaming kids. Horseneck is better."

"What do you think, Ethan?" Jeff asked his brother.

Ethan stretched, raising his arms over his head so that his sleeves fell and showed off his toned biceps. His eyes darted to me before answering. "The girls wear skimpier bikinis at Hampton."

A gagging sound escaped my mouth before I could stop it.

Ethan grinned, obviously delighted to get another rise out of me. "But I'll go wherever Al wants to go. I don't want her to have any reasons to bail on us."

He would twist anything I said, so this time I managed to stay quiet. Nicole met my eyes and I nodded.

"Horseneck it is."

Nicole left with Ethan and Jeff a little while later, all three of them excited about the band playing tonight at The Bean Counter. Ethan had made an impressive effort to convince me to come along, but going to the packed coffee house sounded horrible to me. Thank goodness I had my own car and could use needing to go get us food for the beach as an opt out.

"I'll be over at seven-thirty a.m. sharp!" Nicole hollered from Jeff's jeep as he pulled away.

Right. Sure, she would.

I chuckled as I drove home from the grocery store, remembering Nicole's claim that she'd be ready early. All of our lives I'd had to drag her out the door, kicking and screaming, just to get her to school on time.

I pulled into the driveway, grabbed the bags, and headed up the stairs of the front porch. Twigs snapping in the woods broke through the quiet night. As I looked around to see what might have made the noise, a shiver ran down my spine. The yard was dark, and the porch light didn't reach more than five feet off the steps.

I shook my head, irritated by my paranoia and walked through the front door.

Gram sat on the couch with a crossword book on her lap, and my mother was watching a game show on TV. Pop was slouched in his chair, eyes closed under the half-moon glasses that had slid down low on his nose.

I smiled at them as I quietly set my keys on the sideboard.

At that moment, it wasn't hard to believe that my mother was the happy, carefree girl everyone claimed she was before I was born. The glow from the lamp brightened her partially damp hair. A stranger wouldn't think she was much older than me she looked so young. Even staring at the TV with her mouth slightly open, she was beautiful.

"What time will you be heading to the beach tomorrow?" Gram asked without looking up.

"Nicole says she'll be here at seven-thirty. " I sighed, pulling a cooler out of the closet. "What do you think the odds are of that happening?"

"No comment, Allie-girl," Gram replied, a twinkle in her eye.

Sunlight assaulted my eyelids, and I pulled the blanket up over my head with a groan. I'd been dreaming of cloudy, rain-soaked skies, but judging from the intensity of the sun, there weren't any ominous thunderstorms getting me out of going to the beach today. It was only six o'clock, though, so I climbed out of bed, threw on shorts and a tank top and headed out for a run. At least I'd have a little time to myself.

When I walked back in the house, my mother was already sitting on the couch watching TV. Pop sat at the table reading the Saturday paper. I didn't see Gram anywhere—she was probably out back watering her garden before it got too hot.

"Good morning, Allison," Pop said, folding down the corner of his paper.

"Mornin', Pop," I said as the smell of fresh coffee drew me into the kitchen where my favorite mug already sat on the counter waiting for me. When I returned to the living room, caffeine in hand, Pop continued.

"I hear you kids are heading to the beach today," Pop said, his face hidden behind the newspaper. My mother glanced over at him but quickly looked back to the talk show she was watching.

"That's right. Can't wait." I dropped down on the

couch with my coffee.

Pop folded down the corner of his paper again, peering at me over his reading glasses. "It's okay to have some fun once in a while, Al."

I snorted in response. Going to the beach with Nicole and her friends didn't really count as fun in my book. Other than Nicole, I didn't really feel comfortable around anyone my own age. I'd never fit in, I'd rather just be alone or sit in the backyard with a book while Gram worked in her garden.

"When Beth was a girl, she and Joanne went to the beach just about every weekend during the summer. They were inseparable." Joanne still stopped by to visit at least once a week, so I could believe it. She also happened to be Jeff and Ethan's mother.

I raised an eyebrow. "Are you trying to tell me something, Pop?" I asked with a smirk.

"Nah, sweetheart. Just thinking life is too short, you know? I wouldn't want you to miss out on your share of fun before life gets in the way."

"I'm perfectly happy with a good book and a bowl of Double Fudge ice cream." I grinned widely, trying to show my sincerity, though probably was pushing it toward overkill.

"It sure isn't that you're not pretty enough," he said, ignoring me. "Those eyes of yours are about the bluest I've ever seen. I think all the boys around here are just scared off by your sharp tongue."

"Think so?" I couldn't help laughing as I stood up, patted Pop on the shoulder, and went upstairs to change into my bathing suit.

I glanced at my watch. It was seven forty-five. If
Nicole didn't show up by eight, I was grabbing my book
and camping out in the backyard.

No sooner than the idea crossed my mind, the screen
door slammed. Nicole burst in wearing a hot-pink
terrycloth coverall and flip-flops. Her shoulder-length
blonde hair was pulled up in a high ponytail.

"We're burning daylight here, Al. Let's go!"

"Good morning to you, too. You're practically on
time," I teased.

"It'll be a good morning if you have some coffee left."
She whipped open the cabinet and pulled down a travel
mug. "Mom and Dad aren't even up yet."

I chuckled. "When was the last time you were up at
this hour? I haven't seen you leave the house before nine-
thirty since high school." The hair salon where Nicole
worked at opened at ten o'clock, and she didn't get up
earlier than she had to.

Nicole ignored me and took a long sip of her coffee,
then peered out to the living room. "Whatcha watching,
Aunt Beth?"

"My shows," my mother answered quietly.

I kissed Pop on the cheek and walked over to kiss my
mother on the head. She didn't move, and I gave her a tiny
smile. "Grab the cooler, Nic. I'm going to get the umbrella
and we're outta here."

When the trunk was packed, I slammed it shut just as
Nicole's friend Rachel pulled into the driveway in her tiny

red coupe. She was dressed just like Nicole, only in turquoise, and her curly dark hair was twisted up in an artfully messy bun.

"Hey, girly," she greeted Nicole, not even looking at me. She raised a perfectly shaped brow as she held up her beach tote.

"You'll drive, right, Allison?" Rachel said airily as she tossed her bag into my backseat.

I clenched my teeth. "You bet!"

Jeff pulled his Jeep in behind Rachel's car, and her attention was quickly diverted to sticking her chest out for maximum cleavage exposure."Hey, boys!" she lilted to the three guys in the Jeep.

Nicole caught me as I rolled my eyes. "We're gonna have an awesome day," she stated. "So, don't be a grouch!" She playfully stuck her tongue out and hopped in the car.

I inhaled the salty ocean air, and the lingering scent of suntan lotion filled my nose. The sun was searing my legs, and it was time for a break in the shade. My skin burned easily and although I had sunscreen on, I was already looking a little pink. I put my bookmark between the pages and attempted to brush some of the sand off of my legs as I stood. Lifting my arms, I stretched before retreating to the chair under my umbrella.

Down at the water, I could see Rachel with her arms wrapped around her middle, the wind whipping strands of dark hair into her face. She kept jumping and shrieking when Sean or Ethan stumbled on their boogie boards and splashed her. Ethan caught my gaze and motioned for me to come join them. I laughed as a wave collapsed on top of him and shook my head.

Settling into my spot, I took off my sunglasses and closed my eyes, listening to the sound of the gulls. I sighed contentedly. *This wasn't so bad.*

A loud cawing interrupted my tranquil moment. I pried open an eye and looked at the kids building a sand castle next to our spot. There was a crow standing a few feet away, facing my direction. Weird. I'd never seen a crow at the beach before. Maybe there was a beached seal nearby.

I started to open my book up, but the hairs along the back of my neck stood up, and a funny feeling came over me, like I was being watched. I glanced around, and this time, the crow locked eyes with me. Something about its beady eyes made me shudder, and I turned away quickly.

On my other side, Nicole was just about done burying Jeff in the sand. All that was visible was his spiky brown hair and his Red Sox visor.

"Just stay still for one more second, Jeff. I've got to get a picture," Nicole begged as she grabbed her camera from her towel. She clicked a few times before the sand started to crack and crumble around him.

"That's it, let me out of here!" Jeff shouted. The sand broke apart around him, and he climbed out. Nicole yelped in surprise as he took off chasing her down to the water.

"Come swim with us, Al!" Nicole yelled over her shoulder as she ran.

I shook my head with a smile. "I'm good," I called out before reopening my book.

A few minutes later, I heard a quiet thud as Ethan dropped down to his knees on the blanket by my feet. He dug around the cooler and pulled out a soda.

"Aren't you having fun?" he asked breathlessly between gulps.

"As a matter of fact, I am," I replied, gesturing to the umbrella and my book.

"Yeah? Whatcha reading?"

I felt a blush rise on my cheeks as I held the book out for him to see. I was reading *Gone With The Wind*. Again.

Ethan started laughing, nearly choking on his soda. "I imagined you up here reading *The Guide to Modern Physics*. I would've never guessed you were reading a romance novel!" He stretched himself out on the blanket and closed his eyes to the sun, his lips curved up in that mocking little smile. His dark hair was slicked back with water, and he was perfectly tanned. I couldn't help noticing that his lashes were a thick, dark fringe. I forced myself to look away.

When I glanced back at him—I couldn't help it— Rachel had snuck onto the blanket and gestured to me with her finger to her lips. She flopped down onto her stomach and began running a piece of ice that had fallen out of the cooler along Ethan's chest, causing him to shout in surprise.

"You're going down!" he yelled before hauling Rachel up over his shoulder and running down to toss her, squealing, into the ocean.

I looked down to the water, wondering how Sean felt about Rachel's not-so-subtle display. They had one of those on-again-off-again relationships. They were all friends, but her flirting with Ethan must have bothered him. If I wanted to be honest, it even bothered *me*.

I pushed all of Nicole's friends out of my thoughts and tried to enjoy the rest of the day. When it was time to leave, I walked up the old wooden steps to the parking lot with my arms full of beach gear. The others were lagging behind, but I could still hear the sounds of their laughter and teasing.

"If you're going with Jeff, I am too," I heard Rachel say to Nicole in her whiny voice.

"Sweet! Shotgun in Al's car," Ethan yelled. A smile crept onto my face—Rachel would be disappointed that she wouldn't get to cozy up next to him in the backseat. Good thing no one could see my face.

"Damn, man, I was just going to say that!" Sean said, a *thump* following. I could only imagine from Ethan's grunt that Sean had whacked him upside the head. I laughed to myself that both guys were so desperate to stay away from Rachel.

I opened the hatch and started loading it when Ethan gently pushed me aside. "I got this," he said, winking at me as he hefted the cooler in.

"Yeah, I wouldn't want to break a nail," I muttered, placing my bag in the back.

Ethan just laughed and shook his head.

"Meet us at Nic's!" Jeff shouted out his window before tearing out of the parking lot.

I started the car as Ethan and Sean piled in. As usual, Sean reached up front and ruffled my hair before settling in his seat. He grew up in the house on the other side of Nicole's, and he'd always been nice to me, even if his sometimes-girlfriend was a jerk.

"You coming over tonight?" Ethan asked as he flipped through the CD's in my case.

"Me?" I tried to swallow down the butterflies. "Are you kidding? My bed is already calling my name," I replied, trying to keep an aloof tone.

Ethan shook his head and smirked, no doubt trying not to laugh at me. "We're just going to be watching a movie."

"Didn't your mother teach you not to beg, dude?" Sean asked, teasing. "You probably have a hot date, right Allie-O?" He shook my shoulder lightly. I smiled at the old nickname from the days when we used to play hide-and-seek in our neighborhood.

"Yeah, a hot date with Rhett Butler," Ethan said. I kept my eyes on the road, but I couldn't help the smile that played on my lips.

"Poor Ethan," Sean said. "I think Rachel wants to snuggle with you tonight, pal." He was laughing, but there was an edge to his voice. The idea of Rachel and Ethan together made my chest squeeze, too.

Ethan chuckled. "No, thanks. Rachel is *all* yours. She's not my type."

"Since when do *you* have a type?" Sean asked, the tension lifting.

"I'm twenty-three years old, man. Time to start thinking of the future."

I nearly snorted soda out of my nose…until he slung his arm around the back of my chair. Then it was all I could do to keep the car on the road.

He had to know the way he affected me, how he got under my skin. Four years ago, in one of my weaker moments, I'd fallen for his charm. I couldn't let that happen again. But the memory of that kiss still left me breathless.

I pulled my car into the driveway, thanking the universe for getting me through the trip without too much drama.

The guys grabbed the umbrella and cooler and headed for the house. I shut the trunk and was about to scoop my bag and chair up when a raucous of caws and screeches broke out in the woods.

Startled, I grabbed my things and hurried toward the porch. I watched the tree line as I went, where a handful of large crows were swooping up and down in the yard, knocking leaves and small branches all over the place.

I had almost reached the porch steps when I walked straight into Ethan, who was squinting at the scene the birds were making, too. I stumbled back, nearly falling, and he grabbed my elbow to steady me, sending electricity shooting through my body.

I yanked my arm back as though he'd burned me. He held his hands up, palms facing forward.

"Easy. You all right?" He laughed, and I felt my cheeks flare.

I pushed past him, embarrassed that I'd practically fallen over backward and annoyed that he had laughed at me.

"Hey! Allie..."

I stopped with my hand on the screen door. I didn't know why I was overreacting like this—it wasn't the first time he joked around with me—and it made me even more flustered. I heard his footsteps as he climbed onto the porch behind me and tried to keep my cool. My hand dropped from the door, and I turned around.

Ethan looked at me, his warm brown eyes searching mine. "Don't be mad."

I took a deep breath and looked away. "I'm not mad," I said. "I was just sort of freaked out by the birds." I looked at the spot they'd been tearing up just seconds ago. They were nowhere to be found.

He opened his mouth to speak just as Sean appeared at the screen door. I stood aside to let him out and internally thanked him for saving me from another self-induced awkward moment.

"You sure you can't come over tonight?" Ethan asked, his usual wry expression back in place.

Sean just snorted and gave my shoulder a squeeze as he walked by. "Later, Allie-O."

I shook my head at Ethan. "I'm sure, but thanks for the help carrying the beach stuff inside."

He grinned and nodded. "Well, have fun with Rhett then." He followed Sean toward Nicole's house.

"Did you have a good time today, honey?" Gram said as she pushed the door open and held it for me.

Tearing my gaze away from Ethan, I made myself smile. "Yeah, it was okay."

I brought the bag up to my room and then headed back out to my car. Once I confirmed that there was nobody around, I made my way to the spot where the birds had been. I expected to see a raccoon or opossum lying dead in the woods, but other than scattered leaves and twigs, there was no sign that the birds had even been there. The entire backyard was clear, not even a squirrel in sight.

I walked all the way around the perimeter of the yard until I was satisfied that I was just worrying over nothing. *Of course nothing was out here.* I rubbed my hands over my face. I couldn't help wondering if this was how it had started for my mother—paranoid over every little sound, every strange happening.

I walked past the fence to Nicole's yard and froze when I heard a hushed conversation on the other side.

"Obviously he wants to get with Allison because she's like, *no-man's land.* Once he gets in her pants, he'll lose interest." Rachel said my name like it was acid on her tongue.

"Give me a break, Rach," Nicole replied. I could just imagine her dramatic eye roll.

"What? Isn't she still, like, a virgin or something?" Rachel said, snickering. "She's probably a lesbian anyway."

"I think you need to back off my cousin." Nicole's voice hardened. "Got it?"

When I realized what I was doing, I hurried inside. I did not need to hear any more of that conversation. Time to take a quick shower and read for awhile. That would sort me out.

My mother was perched in her usual spot on the couch as I entered the living room, with Gram and Pop in their seats. The television was on, but when I glanced at my mother, I noticed she wasn't watching it. She was looking out the window. Her expression was blank, but there was a tear trickling down her cheek.

My mother walks through an endless stretch of green forest. There is a man by her side, with big, blue eyes and wavy, caramel hair. She beams up at him. His hand gently rests on her back, steadying her as she steps over fallen branches and stones. His eyes are constantly moving, restless.

Black birds surround them. One swoops down at my mother, and its red eyes glare at her as it drags its talons across her chest. As quickly as it came, it flies off with the rest, leaving her shirt torn and streaked with blood. The man's eyes are wild, searching the forest. He's yelling words I don't understand as he pulls my mother toward him.

I jolted awake, my pajamas soaked in sweat, my breaths coming fast. But it was just another dream. Yet, muffled sobs came from my mother's bedroom across the hall. I climbed out of my bed and hurried to my mother's room.

Her bed was empty, and my chest seized. But when I spun around I saw her in her window seat, staring out at the woods. Relief flooded through me.

"Mom," I whispered, but she didn't move. "Mom, please look at me," I tried again, sitting down on the seat beside her. She turned to face me then. Tears lined her cheeks like silver rivers down her moonlit face.

"Allison," she murmured. I shivered at the clarity in her voice. I hadn't heard her say my name since I was six years old.

"It's okay, Mom." I wiped her tears away with a tissue from the nightstand. Her eyes shone brighter than I'd ever seen them, and they burned holes into mine.

"You look...so much like him." She didn't have to say who she meant. I knew she was thinking about my father.

"I'm sorry if that hurts you," I said, trying to hang onto the moment of lucidity.

"No," she whispered, staring back into my eyes. "Your father was beautiful, just like you."

"Did he hurt you?" I immediately regretted my words—I knew how easy it was to push her over the edge.

My mother shuddered, and just like that, she was gone. Her eyes glazed over, completely void of recognition. She turned her head slowly and stared back out at the woods.

Chapter Three

Sunday morning, I sat at the kitchen table after my run, picking through the newspaper that Pop had already dissected. My mother sat across from me, threading and unthreading her fingers. I picked up my coffee cup and grimaced when I took a sip to find it unexpectedly cold. I walked over to get a warm-up and the doorbell rang.

I glanced around, Gram was out in the garden, and Pop had taken a ride down to the hardware store to do paperwork. I set the coffee pot aside to answer the door. A young man stood on the other side, looking off into the woods. I didn't think I'd ever seen him before, but there was something familiar about him.

"Hello. I'm looking for Beth O'Malley, please," he said with a heavy Irish accent.

"Beth?" Nobody ever came over asking for Beth O'Malley. Then his eyes met mine.

Just like in a movie, when the camera zooms into someone's face and everything else ceases to exist for that moment, my world stopped.

Because I *had* seen those eyes before.

They had gazed affectionately at my mother in my dreams.

His light golden-brown hair was short, but I could tell that if he grew it out a few inches, it would be wavy just like mine. He looked exactly like the photos I had in my room.

"She can't come to the door." The words tumbled out, my heart thrumming in my chest like a thousand butterfly wings. "I'm her daughter, Allison. Can I help you with something?"

"Oh, I see." His brow furrowed, like he didn't actually understand at all. "No. Thank you, Allison. Good day." He turned toward the stairs.

"Wait!" I shouted. "Liam?"

He cleared his throat, froze, and spoke over his shoulder. "Yes. Has she told you about me then?"

"Not really, no."

It was true. I only ever heard his name during her episodes. When I was little, she would sit in her room sometimes holding a piece of paper in her hands and cry. One day I snuck into her bedroom while she was playing her violin and stole the paper—what turned out to be pictures of her and Liam. I thought that if I took away the thing that made her cry, she would be happy with just me.

I shook my head. "She mentioned the name to my grandmother, after she came back from Ireland."

"Right." He turned back to face me again. "Do you suppose I might be able to speak with your mother later?"

I crossed my arms over my chest. "You haven't spoken to her in the past twenty-two years, obviously."

25

"I beg your pardon?" Liam cleared his throat again.

"I said it's obvious you haven't talked to my mother since she came back from Ireland twenty-two years ago."

"Please, you must understand—"

"Oh, I think I understand perfectly. You knocked my mother up and sent her back to the US, and now…what? You're in the neighborhood so you thought you'd drop by to say hello?"

"I don't know what you've been told. But"—he paused, swallowing hard—"I assure you, I knew nothing of a child."

I stepped out onto the porch, quietly shutting the door behind me. I tried to keep my expression calm and indifferent.

I noticed his jaw muscles clenching. Something else we had in common, I guess.

"I don't know what to say," he whispered as he passed a hand through his hair. "I didn't know you existed, yet... here you are."

"Here I am," I laughed, without humor. "I guess you're wondering why I won't let you see my mother?"

"I suppose I am. But I might have a bit of an idea," he said. His blue eyes looked sad and far older than I'd originally thought.

"You think so?" I snapped. "And why might that be?"

"Oh, Allison. I daresay I know far more than I wish to." He sighed and ran his hands through his hair again.

"So, you know that my mother is crazy? That she can't even leave the house without being sedated? Do you know that most days she doesn't say more than ten words? And on those *off* days, she rants and screams your name?" I took a deep breath, my chest heaving with emotion. I had been going for cool and indifferent, but, his innocent act set me off. I couldn't even look at him. "Is that what you wish you didn't know?"

"Won't you let me see her?" he pleaded, his fingers still laced in his hair. "I have loved your mother all these years. I know this is my fault, believe me. There was nothing I could do, but I would have done anything..." His voice trailed off, and there was a faraway look in his eyes.

I was at a complete loss. How could he just show up twenty-two years after tearing my mother's heart apart? How could he stand here, claiming to love her in one breath, and yet say he was helpless to do anything about it in the next?

"Let me guess—you were married, with a kid or two already. I bet the American student and her illegitimate baby didn't fit well in the family portrait, right?" My hands clenched into fists.

Liam laughed then, but it was a cold, terrible laugh. His face clouded over, and for a moment I regretted speaking to him so harshly. I didn't know this guy. I had no idea what he was capable of.

For what must have been the longest two minutes of my life, he didn't say anything. He didn't even look at me, just stared off into space. His eyes were hard and shiny, like marbles, glistening with unshed tears.

"No, I was never married," he finally answered. "I wish it were so simple."

He looked directly into my eyes then, and for a moment I couldn't think of a single thing to say. Questions tumbled through my mind, but there were so many that I had no way of knowing where to begin. I opened my mouth to ask what he meant, but he spoke first.

"I will find a way to undo what has been done, or I will die trying." He took two steps back. "I understand your anger. You're completely justified. But know this—you *will* see me again." He nodded curtly and strode down the front walk. Just like that.

I didn't have to work on Sunday, but I almost wished I had, if only for the distraction. The sky was bright blue as I stepped back out onto the front porch, and I could hear the chords from "Drowsy Maggie" floating out from the den. My mother hadn't played such a peppy tune on her violin in years. I sat on the top step with an ice-cold glass of lemonade, tapping my foot to the melody. Uncle David had mowed that morning, too, so the smell of freshly cut grass added to the illusion of a perfect summer day. Puffy clouds moved swiftly through the sky, matching the speed of the thoughts passing through my mind.

I couldn't bring myself to tell Gram and Pop about Liam showing up. Every time I considered it, I pictured Liam's face—he was so...*young*. Something about him didn't sit right. It wasn't just that he spoke in riddles. It was that his face hadn't changed a bit from the photo strips my mom clung to when I just was five years old.

No. I did the right thing, I encouraged myself. They had enough to deal with, and something told me I should keep his arrival to myself.

I took a sip of my lemonade and looked around the yard. There were no signs of the fighting black birds, at least. It was actually a peaceful day. It was warm but not as hot as it had been the past week. I stretched my legs out and leaned back on my hands, letting the sun warm my face.

My mother's music danced through my head. When I was a very little girl, she would let me choose the music she'd play. I always loved the fast tunes like "Drowsy Maggie." I would watch her bite her bottom lip in concentration as she moved through each piece. She withdrew completely when I was around seven years old, though, and I missed turning the sheet music for her and dancing along to the reels.

I opened my eyes, and lights sparkled across my vision. I looked down, letting my eyes adjust. Once I could see normally I stood, figuring I should probably do a load of laundry before Gram had a chance to do it for me. But to my left, I saw a twinkling silver light. I turned to walk up the stairs, and sure enough, the same light caught my eye, even when I faced the house.

I remembered Gram would sometimes hang aluminum pie plates near her vegetable garden to keep the birds away. I must have not been paying attention when I walked past her gardens—surely she had put some out.

The rumbling of an engine announced Jeff's arrival next door and jerked me away from my thoughts. I looked over to see Nicole bouncing down the driveway. She glanced over at me, her face all lit up.

"There you are! I've been texting you all morning." She signaled to Jeff that she'd be just a minute and made her way over to me.

I sighed, knowing what was going to happen before she was even in front of me. Once again, I had no believable excuses.

"I'm going to a cookout at Jeff's parents' house. Wanna come?" No matter how many times I'd turned down her invitations in the past, she never lost hope that I would one day be happy to tag along with her and her friends.

"I have laundry to do, Nic," I mumbled as I walked into the house, wincing when I heard her follow behind me. She would never give up so easily.

"And, it will be here tomorrow, won't it?"

My mother was still playing her violin in the den. Her talent never faded, no matter how ill she became. As I walked past, I could see Gram coming in through the sliding door. She was wearing her gardening hat and gloves, the knees of her pants caked with soil.

"Hello, girls." Gram smiled at us as she pulled the gloves off, wiping her brow.

"Hey, Gram," Nicole said, grinning. "Aunt Beth is doing okay, isn't she?"

Gram looked between the two of us, a knowing smile forming on her face. She licked her lips and laughed.

"Aunt Beth is just fine, why do you ask?"

I widened my eyes at Gram. She usually helped me fend off Nicole's endless invitations.

"Great, so you can come, Al!"

"Are you sure I'm even invited?" I knew I was just putting off the inevitable. But I had to put up a little bit of a fight. I couldn't let Nicole get complacent.

She glanced at me and frowned. "I *just* invited you."

I breathed deeply. "If I come, will you leave me alone

for the rest of the week?"

Her dismissive expression made me laugh. "Yeah, sure. Let's go. This will be so much fun," she said, sounding much more excited than I felt.

I made a "how could you?" face at Gram and followed after my cousin. I would never let Nicole know, but the idea of being surrounded by mindless conversation might actually be the only way I could make it through this day.

The Magliaro family never had small get-togethers. They were a huge Italian family with plenty of relatives and friends constantly stopping by unannounced. A cookout there meant three times as many people around as there usually were. Luckily, their house was enormous.

It stood a mile back from the road, and I sat in the back of Jeff's Jeep, bumping and bouncing all the way up the long, snaking driveway. Half a dozen cars were already there when we arrived. Jeff pulled right onto the front lawn and secured the parking brake.

I followed them into the house, smiling at relatives I'd met before, even if I couldn't remember their names. The air was thick with the smell of spicy Italian cooking. Two booming male voices were having a friendly argument about which Patriots tight end should be starting in the fall, and little kids were running around, darting under our feet.

"Eli, what did I tell you about running inside Auntie Joanne's house?" Jeff mock-scolded a dark-haired boy as he ran by. The boy grinned up at him, showing several missing teeth, and scooted out the front door.

In the kitchen, Joanne was putting chips into bowls and chatting with an older woman. The second she saw me and Nicole, her eyes lit up, and she excused herself before rushing for us.

"Hello, girls! So glad to see you," she said before turning to Jeff. "Did you offer them anything to drink Jeff?"

"Uh, not yet, Ma. We just got here."

Joanne made shooing motions to her son, and he threw up his arms before going off in search of drinks.

She leveled me with her eyes. "How's your mom, honey?"

"You know…same old." I put on my best polite smile.

Joanne nodded, her face showing that she saw right through me. "Well, I'm sorry I haven't stopped by in a few days. I'll come by soon, I promise."

I nodded. I knew she would.

She gave my arm a gentle pat and then excused herself as Jeff came back with two bottles of water. I took one from him and caught sight of Ethan across the family room. My smile faltered a bit—he was leaning against the back of the sofa, whispering into the ear of a redhead who looked vaguely familiar.

Nicole cleared her throat. "Whatcha looking at, Al?"

I scowled at her as my cheeks heated up. "I'm not looking at anything," I said, looking down at my flip flops.

I snuck a peek back at Ethan, who was laughing and standing inappropriately close to the girl. Then I remembered: she went to high school with us.

"Hey, man." Sean came up, clapping his hand on Jeff's

shoulder. Behind him, Rachel stood watching Ethan talk to the redhead, too.

"Hey. We still on for some Home Run Derby?" Jeff asked, curling his arm around Nicole's waist.

I glanced back at Ethan. *Lisa*, that was her name.

Sean grinned. "Of course I am. Let's do this!"

"Hey, Ethan," Jeff hollered across the room. "Get your hands out of Lisa's pants, and let's go play ball!"

Nicole smacked him and Joanne shot him a look, but Jeff and Sean just cracked up. They weren't the least bit sorry.

Ethan separated himself from Lisa and walked over to where we all stood, his smile wicked. Sean punched him in the shoulder.

"What? We were just catching up." Ethan's teeth gleamed against his deep tan as he laughed. I stared back down at my feet again, wishing I were home doing laundry.

"Hey, Al." Ethan said, turning his grin on me. I attempted to make my face completely unreadable.

Dammit. Why did I always have to react to him?

"Hey," I said, trying for indifference but only achieving awkwardness.

"Come on, come on." Jeff let go of Nicole and nudged Ethan toward the back door.

While the guys were playing ball I sat on the deck with Nicole, Rachel, and a few of their other friends, and listened to them talk about who was dating whom and who was pregnant with whose kid. I recognized the tone of Rachel's voice every time she spoke. The same one she'd used when she'd called me no-man's land and decided I was a lesbian.

This was the kind of the thing I avoided. Playing Home Run Derby sounded way better than listening to gossip from Nic's snooty friends. I stood, kicked off my flip flops and headed off the deck, ignoring Nicole calling my name.

Ethan stood with a wiffle ball in his hands, his expression intrigued. "You playing?"

I glanced back at the girls on the deck watching me and shrugged. "Count me in."

Sean jogged over with the bat and held it out for me, grinning. He knew I'd played softball and run track all through high school to pad my transcripts. And I was no slouch at either sport. "Pick your pitcher, Allie-O."

The smirk on Ethan's face was a challenge, and I couldn't resist. "Ethan has the ball. He can pitch to me."

"I hope you haven't gotten rusty," Ethan said. He made a big show of stretching and winding up before he finally tossed the ball to me.

I swung and smacked it over the pool house, and Sean started shouting and cheering. Ethan shook his head, but he was smiling. He clearly thought I would be an easy out.

But no. I made it all the way to the final round, kicking Sean and Jeff out of the game.

"You gonna let her win, E?" Jeff called, winking at me from the picnic table where he sat drinking a beer.

Ethan chuckled, showing off those damn dimples. He looked down at the ball in his hands and then back up at me. "If I do, will you let me take you out?"

"What? Like on a date?" I snorted, trying to look braver than I felt. "Not a chance."

"Wait a sec…I like this. Let's make a wager," he said.

The guys were all hooting and hollering at me, my face no doubt crimson. I bit my lip, feeling all their eyes on me. "What do I get if I win?"

"I'm thinking, hang on." He held up his finger, his brow furrowed in thought. His eyes widened with excitement, and I knew I would regret whatever he had to say.

"If I win, I get a kiss." If it was possible, my cheeks flushed even more. Cue the laughter and the cat calls.

"And, if *I* win?" I said, setting a hand on my hip to stop the shaking.

He looked at me for a second, considering. "If you win, I won't ever ask you out again."

The idea earned a chorus of "Yeah, right" and "No way" from the guys.

My mouth fell open. I had not been expecting that, but his expression was serious. The laughing around us fell away for a second, and I could only stare at him, feeling the color drain from my face. His expression remained solemn, and he met my gaze head on.

I nodded stiffly and swallowed. "All right."

His grin came back in full force. "Oh, and Al?" I raised my eyebrows at him. "I won't lose."

He was right. I swung at his third pitch and completely missed. And when it was his turn, he smacked the first ball I pitched a hundred yards past the mark.

I couldn't help but laugh at his victory dance—his hips

swinging, fists rotating over his head. His energy was contagious. He bounded toward me, a grin on his face.

"Told you," he said.

I shrugged, about to make some kind of snide remark when Joanne shouted from the deck.

"Food's ready!"

When it was time to go, the nervous feeling in my stomach intensified, and I almost regretted eating so much. This wouldn't be the first time I'd kissed Ethan Magliaro; I knew what he was capable of.

It's just a stupid kiss, I repeated over and over in my head. I could get through it, and then everything would go back to normal. Then my long-lost father's face flashed in my mind. Okay, as normal as possible. Nothing had to change because of one little kiss.

When Nicole asked Jeff to bring her home, I stood to join them, but Ethan shot me an "oh, no you don't" look. I hadn't really expected to get out of the bet, but I didn't want to appear eager, either. That would only make things worse. He grabbed my hand, and pulled me toward his truck, while my cousin and his brother left us to drive back to Gram's alone. I waved at Joanne without meeting her eyes, knowing she probably knew all about our little wager.

He opened the passenger door for me and waited until I was settled before closing it. He came around and slid in next to me. He didn't start the engine right away, though. We sat in silence in his parents' driveway.

Ethan finally looked over at me, his forehead crinkling in concern. "You know I'm not going to force you to do anything you don't want to do, right?"

A nervous laugh escaped. "You won the bet."

Ethan laughed and shook his head as he started the truck. He headed toward the road, and the silence stretched between us. We didn't speak, but he kept looking over at me with an undefinable expression on his face.

I had spent more than my share of time watching Ethan's face. I'd watched him play hockey, I'd watched him play baseball. I'd watched as he flirted with girls, I'd watched him stand stoically at his grandfather's funeral. I thought I knew how to read him pretty well. But at that moment, I couldn't figure out what was going through his mind.

My phone vibrated in my pocket. I pulled it out and checked the number. *Nicole.*

"Don't freak out, but I just—"

"Nicole!" I couldn't help raising my voice. Sometimes she could be so exasperating. I hadn't even gotten home yet, and she was already drilling me.

"Wait, Al, listen – it's your mother. Gram and Pop had to take her to the hospital. She'll be okay, but she needed to get stitches."

My heart stuttered in my chest. "Stitches? What happened?"

"I don't really know. Mom just said she had an episode during dinner and was banging on the window...and the glass broke."

I looked over and Ethan met my eyes curiously.

"We're almost home, meet me there." I clicked my

phone shut and leaned my head against the back of the seat. "My mom broke a window with her hand. She needs stitches."

I looked over at Ethan, expecting to see pity, but, thankfully he just nodded and kept driving.

"Do you want me to take you to the hospital?" he asked, his voice gentle.

"You don't mind?"

Ethan clenched his jaw, and I looked away. "Of course I don't mind. You should probably text Nicole and let her know, though."

We drove the rest of the way in silence, a million feelings—namely guilt—running through my mind. I should have been there. I should never have gone out. But what would it have mattered if I was there? Would I have been able to help? Oh god, did Liam show up again? I was starting to hyperventilate.

Ethan placed a hand on my knee as he parked the car, and for once, my heart rate slowed rather than raced. "She'll be okay," he said.

I nodded, and then we hurried into the emergency department, scanning the crowded lobby. I didn't see my grandparents anywhere, so I headed to the Triage station where a middle-aged woman was typing something into the computer. She didn't even look up when I arrived. I bounced on the balls of my feet for a second, waiting for her to greet me. Finally, I coughed to get her attention.

She glanced up at me. "Can I help you?" she asked, her voice nasally.

"Yes, my mother is here—Elizabeth O'Malley. I need to know where I can find her."

"Just a minute." She yawned and typed a few strokes into her keyboard.

I looked over at Ethan to find him watching me, his expression anxious. As I turned my attention back to the woman at the desk, I saw Pop walking toward us, carrying two coffees.

"Thanks, I'm all set," I said to the receptionist. She returned my gaze with a bland expression.

"Allison, what are you doing here?" Pop asked, glancing between me and Ethan.

"Nic called and said you had to bring Mom in for stitches, so Ethan drove me over. How is she? Is she okay?"

He smiled tiredly. "She'll be fine. Twelve stitches in her left hand. Those darn birds in the yard were making an awful racket. She was really upset." Pop shook his head and motioned for us to follow him.

"Al, do you want me to take off?" Ethan asked. "I can stay if you want me to."

I looked at him. "You can go. I'll be fine."

He shoved his hands in his pockets and looked out the huge glass window in the lobby. "Okay, well, let me know if you need anything."

I smiled and nodded. "Thanks for bringing me, Ethan. I owe you."

The corner of his mouth lifted. That was a look I recognized. "I'll keep that in mind."

Chapter Four

Gram was sitting at the table with a clipboard when I walked into the kitchen the next morning, remaking the chart that kept track of my mother's medication schedule. She now had to add painkillers to the anti-psychotic drugs she already took daily.

I watched my grandmother fill in the sheet, whispering to herself about the dosages and medication names. I wondered, not for the first time, if I'd actually be able to handle the medications and care of my mother on my own.

I pulled my hair back into a ponytail. I had to work the ten o'clock shift at the hardware store. My grandfather wasn't working that morning, but I didn't see him around the house. Then the sight of the plastic covering the window in the living room gave me a pretty good idea where he was.

I poked my head into the den to check on my mother. The sight of the bandage on her hand wasn't what upset me most. She just sat there in a chair, staring at the trees. Pain was written in the tight lines around her mouth and eyes.

Knowing she was on pain meds, I guessed it wasn't something physical.

I cleared my throat quietly, letting her know I was in the room. At first I didn't think she'd look at me, but after several heartbeats she turned her head toward me. A tiny gasp escaped before I could cover my mouth with my palm. Her eyes were vacant and dull, but it didn't mask her misery. I had never seen her so despondent.

I made my way into the room and sat on the sofa across from her. She shifted her gaze back toward the window. I wished I knew what went on in her mind when she was like this. Maybe then I could help. Was she thinking about Liam? How would she react if she actually saw him again?

The screen door creaked from the porch, and I heard my grandfather's voice. And then Ethan's...

From where I sat I could see him walk in carrying a new window. He was dressed for work in his hunter green Magliaro Construction T-shirt. The muscles in his forearms were taut as he brought the window into the living room. The door slammed, and my grandfather followed.

With a small sigh, I rose and tiptoed out of the den, leaving my mother still staring out into the woods. I grabbed my keys from the sideboard in the living room as Ethan measured the frame of the window with a tape measure, a pencil stuck between his lips. I smiled at how boyish he looked.

"I'm off to work." I walked over to the table in the kitchen and placed my hand gently on Gram's back and kissed her hair.

"Oh, honey. Did you get something to eat?" She

pushed her papers away and looked up at me with a frown.

"I'll just grab something on my break." I smiled to reassure her, even though I knew better.

"Give me just one minute. I'll pack you a lunch."

"If it will make you feel better, I'll come home for lunch?" I met her gaze, wishing she wouldn't worry about me so much.

Gram's frown smoothed. "That'd be good."

I shook my head and sighed, but I was still smiling in spite of myself. I turned to leave, and Ethan met my eyes, his expression unsure.

"How's your mom today?"

I twisted the end of my ponytail, "She seems okay," I said. "Thanks for helping with the window."

Ethan looked down at the floor. For a second I thought he might be embarrassed but when he looked up his roguish smile set my cheeks on fire.

"My pleasure, Allison."

The look on his face spread the blush down my neck, and I hurried toward the front door. As I walked out, I could still feel Ethan watching me.

"Which color would you go with, Allison?"

I looked up from the ordering screen on the computer to see Gus Baker holding two strips of paint chips up for me, frown lines etched between his winged eyebrows. I took a deep breath before walking over to the counter where Gus stood waiting for me, his watery blue eyes watching me. From across the counter, I could smell the tang of dirty laundry and decaying teeth.

I tried not to be annoyed at the little old man, but Gus was in here *every day.* I guess he was lonely, but he spent as much time in this store as I did. And he never bought anything.

"I'd go with the eucalyptus green," I said in my friendliest voice.

"I just don't know. There are so many of these colors! How does anyone choose?" Gus grumbled, his eyes intent on my face.

I swallowed, forcing my smile to stay in place as I breathed through my mouth. I just wanted to get the big order that just came in all set for Pop, but Gus had been here for the past forty-five minutes comparing shades of green. I sighed inwardly. He needed to find a new hangout.

The door jingled, signaling a new arrival. I glanced at the door. Ethan. Figures.

Seeing me, his eyes lit up and his face broke into a stomach-twisting half-smile. I shook my head at him, and he chuckled. He knew the effect that grin had on girls, obviously.

Gus's rumbly throat-clearing brought me back to reality. He was still watching me, waiting for my reply as though his life depended on it.

"Maybe going with green is a bad idea, after all," Gus said. "I guess I'll just keep it the way it is."

I nodded and closed my eyes to hide my exasperation. When I reopened them, Ethan was standing a few aisles back, toying with the foam paintbrushes. His smirk stayed firmly in place, his dimples doing a number on my willpower.

"You know," Gus said. "I've heard the lunch special down at The Pickle Barrel includes a meal for two for ten dollars. I would really like to treat you sometime. You're such a big help to me here."

I opened my mouth in shock, staring back at Gus without replying. I could hear snickering from the paintbrush aisle and glared in Ethan's direction as he coughed to cover up his amusement.

I had to say something, but words wouldn't come. Gus just looked at me with his cloudy eyes wide and hopeful.

"Hey, how's it going Gus?" Ethan sauntered over and clapped Gus on the back. I cocked my head at him in confusion.

"Oh," Gus sputtered. "Hey, there yourself, Ethan. How's the family?"

Everyone knew everyone in this town. You couldn't go anywhere without someone asking about your family.

"Doing well, thanks. I'm just popping in to bring my girl her lunch." He grinned and held out a little brown lunch sack. My eyes widened with surprise. *Now what is he doing?*

"Your girl, huh?" Gus looked between Ethan and me, his expression crestfallen. "Well, that's great." Gus stared at me a minute longer before muttering something about seeing me later and shuffling toward the exit.

"You're welcome," Ethan said, waggling his eyebrows at me.

"Who said I was *your girl*?" I huffed, placing my hands on my hips. I tried to be serious but a laugh escaped. The relief of avoiding turning down Gus's invitation kept my annoyance at Ethan's remark at bay.

Ethan placed the lunch sack on the counter and leaned forward on his palms. "Just having a little fun."

I rolled my eyes at him.

"How long have you had poor Gus smitten?" Ethan was still leaning forward, his big brown eyes glowing with humor.

"*Poor Gus* is just lonely. He's in here just about every day."

Ethan shook his head and placed a hand over his heart. "I know how he feels. The poor sap."

"So, what are you *really* doing here, besides saving Gus from heartache?" I asked, heading back to the computer and perching myself on the stool to work on the order.

"After I put in the window, your grandmother asked me to bring this down....to save you having to come home for lunch."

I snorted, keeping my eyes on the screen.

"And, I don't intend on forgetting our little wager." He straightened and crossed his arms, daring me to protest.

I laughed. "What, here? While I'm at work?" I avoided his eyes. Many girls had gotten lost in those eyes, but I knew better.

"What time do you get off work?" he asked.

I turned and narrowed my eyes at him. "I close at six. Then I have to balance the register, so around six thirty."

Ethan looked down at his hands for a second, then glanced up at me through his thick lashes. "You want to get something to eat when you're done?"

I licked my lips, his dark brown eyes pulling me in. I

tore my gaze away and tried to focus on the computer screen. He didn't say anything for a few moments, and I fidgeted, knowing he was watching me. When I turned toward him, his expression was so intense that my stomach somersaulted.

"Just one time," he said quietly.

"What?"

"Say yes, just one time." Ethan slowly moved behind the counter, his eyes never leaving mine.

"If you don't have a good time, fine. But, I've been trying to get you to give me a chance for years. Don't act like you didn't know."

I shook my head slightly as he approached, wanting him closer but afraid of what it would mean.

He stopped, his brow creasing. "I won't hurt you," he whispered.

His expression was so earnest my mind went blank for a moment.

"Ethan," I began, my thoughts scrambled. "You know I'd like to—"

"So say yes."

I looked up at the ceiling. I was tired of always pushing him away. If I went out with him once, maybe then I could convince him too that this was a bad idea. I covered my face with my hands. "All right," I mumbled through my fingers.

"What was that?" I felt the warmth of Ethan's hands as he pulled my own away from my face.

"I said *all right*," I repeated, my insides fluttering.

He gathered my hands and pulled them close to his chest. His scent, clean and fresh like sun-warmed denim, made my knees go weak.

With his head tilted back, he exclaimed in a mock reverent tone, "Yes! Thank you! Six-thirty on the dot. Be ready. I'm picking you up!"

"Cut it out. Don't make me change my mind." I laughed, pulling my hands away.

"Oh, no. You can't back out now!"

I ushered him toward the door. "Ha! Watch me!" I couldn't believe I was flirting back—it went against everything I was trying to do.

But it felt surprisingly good.

I was in big trouble.

Even on weeknights, Inland Seafood was always packed. The smell of fried clams and french fries would be on our skin for a week, but the food was so worth it.

Dinner was the easy part—I could sit across a table from Ethan just fine and make mundane conversation. But when Ethan and I walked to his truck, all I could feel was the heavy air between our swinging arms. Then he stopped in front of the ordering window at Dee Dee's Ice Cream Parlor and looked over at me expectantly.

My eyebrows shot up. "What?"

He laughed, showing his dimples. "Were you really gonna walk past *ice cream* without demanding some?"

I felt the warmth rise up my neck. "I do have self-control, you know."

"So I see." He snorted. "But *I* want ice cream. You

don't mind, do you?" His smile glinted in the bright lights outside the ice-cream window.

"Ice cream's fine," I shrugged, trying for nonchalance.

After we each had a cone in hand, we walked straight to his truck. Ethan opened the door for me, but when I moved to climb in, he put his arm across the doorway. I glanced back at him, confused.

"Actually, let's sit on the tailgate and eat these," he said, yanking a quilt out from behind the passenger seat. He handed me his ice cream and opened the tailgate. After he laid the quilt down, he glanced over at me, mischief clear on his face. Before I had a chance to question him, he hoisted me up onto the tailgate. I yelped in protest, but it was no use.

"It's a perfect night," he said, jumping up next to me and grabbing his ice cream. His arm brushed my bare shoulder, igniting my skin where he touched me. I inhaled sharply, breathing in his scent.

"The stars are all out tonight. There's the Big Dipper," I said, pointing with my free hand. I had to keep talking, even if I was just babbling, so that I wouldn't think about how close he was.

"Allison?" His voice was soft and serious, sounding warning bells in my mind.

"Mm-hmm?" I was afraid to look at him, afraid of the way he said my name, so I kept looking at the sky.

"I want to know why you never date," he said.

I opened my mouth, but I couldn't come up with an appropriate answer so I closed it.

"You could have anyone you wanted. Why is it you're always alone?" I could feel his eyes on me as I stared into the star-studded night.

"Anyone I wanted? That's a little excessive."

"Come on, I'm being serious."

I sighed, trying to think of the right response, one he would understand. "I guess I'm just always busy."

He chuckled. "Everyone is busy. You have to give me a better reason than that."

My mouth felt like cotton. Why did I have such a hard time forming coherent sentences when he was looking at me like that? I licked my lips and looked over at him. He stared directly into my eyes, the question still hanging between us.

"I want to take care of my mother. It's all I want. So, I need to make that happen." I curled my fingers into fists and pulled my shoulders back, looking back up at the stars. I'd had this conversation countless times with Nicole over the years.

"I know you do," he said softly. I glanced back at him, surprised he wasn't telling me that what I wanted was ridiculous. "But...who will take care of you?"

"I will take care of me." I shook my head sadly. "My whole life everyone has had to take care of me. My grandparents, my aunt and uncle. They all sacrificed so much for me."

"You act like it's your fault, but it's not."

Now I was back in familiar territory. "My mother was *normal* before I was born, Ethan. When I came along she began her descent into schizophrenia. You don't think that's connected?"

He shifted in his seat. "I just know sometimes things happen, things that can't be explained. But you still deserve to be happy."

I glanced over at him before looking down at my hands. I uncurled my fingers. "I am happy. I'm enrolling in grad school, working and saving the money I make at the store. It's what I want."

"But what about friends? What about fun?"

"My idea of fun is just different from yours, I guess. I don't need to be with a lot of people to be happy." I hoped he would pick up the double entendre of my answer.

Ethan sighed and turned his body to face mine. He reached up and lightly traced a finger down my cheek. A shiver ran through my body. I turned my face away and focused my attention on finishing my ice cream. There were people everywhere. I didn't want anything that happened between me and Ethan to be the subject of town gossip.

"Thanks for coming tonight," Ethan said, unaffected. He reached down and picked up my left hand, interlacing his strong fingers with mine. "It seems like I've been trying to get you to go out with me forever."

I stared down at our joined hands, too shocked to move. "Ethan, you've never had a lack of dates. I'd even say you've had more than your fair share."

He ducked his head and laughed. "You think I'm a jerk, don't you?"

I looked at him and smiled. "No. I don't, actually. What you did today, for my grandparents… that was really great. Thank you."

"You're welcome. It was no big deal." He squeezed my hand and jumped down from the tailgate. "I'm going to take you home now, while you still think I'm so great."

A girl stands in a poorly lit room. There are no windows or lights, but behind her, a flashlight beam brightens the loose dirt beneath her feet. When the girl turns in the direction of the light, it's my face that illuminates. The man holding the flashlight is huge, wearing a tight, black T-shirt, black cargo pants, and enormous black leather boots. His head is shaved like a soldier's, his expression grim. He looks around, and my eyes follow. Broken-down wooden shelves line the stone walls, each one holding all manner of dusty glass jars and bottles, some broken and lying on their sides. It looks like a cellar of some kind.

Liam appears, placing his hand on the wall as blinding light fills the room. I turn to look at the big man, eyes wide. He gestures for me to go after Liam, who has disappeared into the wall of light.

I walk into a large, bright room. The ceiling and walls are rounded, like they are in an enormous dome, something straight out of a fairy tale. I notice an oversized wooden table in the center of the room, where a glass ball the size of a fish bowl sits. It shimmers and glitters from within. I walk toward it, almost as if I'm under a spell. When I reach out to touch the orb Liam grabs my arm and shakes his head. I look up at him, disappointed. I can't tell what he's saying but his lips move as he pulls my arm away from it. Inside the glass ball, suspended in a sparkling prison is a tiny black-haired woman.

I sat up in my bed—*another strange dream*—and sighed in relief to find myself in bed at Gram's. But as my heart settled, I considered how many dreams like that I'd had in the past six months. A whisper in the back of my mind taunted me. *Crazy. Just like her.*

I couldn't remember if my mother's illness began with bizarre dreams, though. The days before my mother really lost her sanity were hazy at best. Memories of her in the mirror combing my hair were outnumbered by the breakdowns and vacant stares.

I look over at my clock. It was early but there was no way I'd be able to get back to sleep. Might as well get my run in before the heat became unbearable.

The rhythmic thumping of my sneakers soothed me when my mind worked overtime. I had always been fast, so fast I sometimes felt like I was flying. It had won me countless medals and awards over the years, but that's not why I did it. Running was something that was for me and only me. Things like schizophrenic mothers, reappearing fathers, and boys with dimples didn't exist when I ran. All I felt was the wind and my heartbeat, my feet carrying me along. And the less I felt right then, the better.

I wiped the sweat from my brow as I got closer to home, my heart pumping, each beat throbbing in my ears. My body felt strong, but inside I felt weak, scared, overwhelmed. I needed to cool down—in more ways than one—so I slowed my pace, trying to match my breaths to my footsteps. Anger at Liam was sitting heavy on my chest, a cannonball filled to the brim with years of guilt and hurt threatening to implode. Why did he have to show up? My mother was sick enough already.

As I approached my grandparents' driveway, a flash of black caught my attention. Those damn black birds had been watching me whenever I came or went. They hadn't caused any more upsets with my mother, at least, so I tried to ignore their beady little eyes, even though I wanted to chase them all away.

I pulled my ear buds out as one flapped its wings. But it was a movement beyond the bird that startled me.

Several yards in from the street I could just make out the figures of two men standing by a pickup truck in the clearing. They were on my grandparents' property, so I edged closer to the tree line to see what they were up to. Through the branches I could see one of the men gesturing with his arms. I couldn't make out their words, but I easily recognized the rich, low voice. Ethan.

What is he doing here? I squinted to identify the man he was talking to, but Ethan's frame obstructed my view. I moved up the path to get a better look.

And when I did my jaw just about hit the dirt.

The man in front of Ethan was a few inches shorter, one hand rested in his light-brown hair, as if it helped him concentrate on what Ethan was saying. I'm not sure what gave me away, but those sharp blue eyes quickly shifted to where I stood. What was Liam doing here talking with Ethan?

As I began backing away, Ethan followed my father's eyes, nailing me in place. His entire demeanor changed upon seeing me there. One minute he was all business, the next his eyes brightened like he was a man in the desert and I was a cold drink of water.

Ethan started toward me, and I was filled with dread as my father walked alongside him, both pairs of eyes trained on my face.

"Hey, Al," Ethan said.

I did my best to smile at him, but my attention was on the man walking to his left.

"I didn't even know your grandparents sold this plot," Ethan said as he approached.

My eyes darted to Liam. This was news to me, too.

"This is Liam McKeown. Liam, this is Allison O'Malley—Tom and Jane's granddaughter."

I nodded politely, and Liam cleared his throat. Being around Liam and Ethan at the same time wasn't something I'd anticipated, and obviously neither did Liam. The tension between us was palpable. When Ethan's cell phone went off, the air in my chest heaved itself out. I couldn't hold my tongue for much longer. He held up his finger and walked a few yards away to take the call.

"What's going on? What are you doing here?" I hissed, glancing over at Ethan who was laughing heartily into the phone.

"Well," Liam began, not meeting my eyes. "I've just bought this lovely piece of land, and I've hired the Magliaros to build a house for me."

"What kind of game are you playing?" My voice was much louder than I'd meant it to be. Ethan looked over his shoulder at me, holding his index finger up.

Liam sighed. "We all have to have a home, don't we?"

Anger licked at the base of my neck. "I won't let you hurt my mother again."

"Easy now, Allison." The sad expression from the first time we met reappeared. "I'm not going to hurt your mother. In fact, I think I can help her. I just need a little more time."

My jaw clenched as cold fear gripped my heart at the memory of mother's tear-streaked face staring out the window. She was so beautiful, so fragile. She would shatter like hand-blown glass if Liam made an appearance in her life. I just knew it.

Ethan hung up the phone and start back to us. "You don't know what you'll do to her if she sees you," I said quickly.

Ethan looked between Liam and me, puzzled, as he stopped beside us.

"Everything okay, Al?"

"Everything is just fine, my friend," Liam answered, his smile reappearing. "Ms. O'Malley and I have just learned we have a lot of the same interests. Isn't that right?"

I swallowed down the first reply that came to mind and glanced down at the ground. Then, looking at Ethan, I put my mask back in place. "Yeah, it seems that way."

Ethan cocked his eyebrow at me and turned to his new client.

"Thanks for meeting with me today, Ethan," Liam said evenly. "I'll be in touch with your office to make arrangements."

Ethan and I stood quietly as Liam walked down the path toward the road.

"What just happened here? It sounded like you were arguing."

"I was taken by surprise, that's all." I smiled, hoping to be convincing. "I had no idea someone had bought this plot." I looked back down the path after Liam. The only vehicle on sight was Ethan's pickup truck. How had Liam gotten here? And what on earth was he up to?

Chapter Five

I ran my finger over the clingy, green tank top hanging in my closet. It was a little revealing for a Fourth of July cookout. *Maybe I should wear a simple T-shirt.* I stood pondering my outfit, focusing on something I could control for a change. Why was I so worried about how I looked for this cookout anyway? I'd known the Magliaros forever. I'd known Ethan forever.

I sighed and reached for the green tank when a flash in the woods stole my attention. There was no way that was just the sun reflection off an aluminum pie plate. I walked over to the window and saw...*nothing.* What was wrong with me? I let out a frustrated groan, threw on my top, and jogged down the stairs. I was going to find those pie plates hanging from trees in the backyard—there was no other explanation for it.

I walked out back, my eyes scanning the trees. I heard footsteps behind me and whipped around, my hand flying to my mouth when I saw my mother standing directly in front of me. She stared over my shoulder into the woods, her gaze intent. She must've seen it too.

"Mom? What are you doing out here?" I asked, looking around for my grandparents. My mother only left the house to go to doctor's appointments, and even then she had to be heavily medicated. She didn't answer me, just kept looking beyond me into the woods where Liam and Ethan had met the other day.

"What is it?" I asked turning back toward the tree line. I bit my lip, hoping she hadn't glimpsed Liam that day.

My mother started walking toward the trees. *Oh, no. Not a good idea.* I rushed up beside her. "Uh, why don't we go back inside, Mom? I think The Ellen Show is coming on."

She stopped and turned to me. She stared into my eyes for a minute, her expression full of longing, then she nodded, the light in her eyes flickering out as she allowed me to lead her toward the deck.

As we climbed the stairs Gram opened the slider, still holding a dishrag in her hand. "There you two are," she said, casting me a curious glance.

"We were just listening to some animals squabbling in the woods, Gram. But we're heading in now since we don't want to miss Ellen." I raised my eyebrows and hoped Gram caught my *I'll tell you later* look.

"Oh, I see," Gram said, nodding.

After I got my mother situated in front of the television, I joined Gram at the kitchen counter where she was chopping a cucumber and adding it to a salad.

"I heard something in the woods," I explained. "I guess Mom followed me outside."

Gram continued chopping. "Hmm…that's strange.

Was there anything out there?"

"Just some birds squabbling," I said, grabbing a cucumber slice. "But that reminds me. Ethan told me he's building a house on that empty plot?"

Gram placed the knife on the counter and wiped her hands on a towel. She looked into my eyes and smiled. It wasn't a happy smile, but a silent plea for understanding.

"You're wondering why Pop and I didn't tell you about selling the property. I understand."

"I know it's none of my business, but it was just a surprise."

"No, of course, it's your business. That land was supposed to be your mother's, just like the property on the other side belongs to Aunt Jessie," she said. "Pop and I talked it over, and we decided to sell it to Mr. McKeown. He paid more than twice what we asked for it, and we're putting the profit in an account for your mother's future."

I nodded and smiled. They had tried to give the land to me after my high school graduation. I hadn't wanted it then, and I didn't want it now. Their plan was definitely a good use for it. But the fact that Liam was the one to instigate it shot off major warning bells in my mind. But I couldn't tell her that…

"Is this for me to bring to the cookout?" I asked, changing the subject.

She glanced up at me, then continued chopping. "It is."

"I don't have to go, if you and Pop want to instead," I offered. "You guys are always cooped up here."

Gram placed the knife on the counter again and turned to look me in the eye. "Don't be silly, Allison." She bent to pull a box of plastic wrap out of the bottom drawer.

"I'm not!" I laughed, knowing exactly what I was doing, but continuing anyway. "I don't mind staying home. Cookouts aren't really my thing."

"You're going to that party, and you'll have a good time. I don't want to hear another thing about it."

The driveway at the Magliaro house was twice as full as it had been for the last cookout. There were even cars parked down the street. Nicole had warned me that in addition to family and co-workers, several of the Magliaro's clients would be there too, networking opportunity that it was. She saved a spot for me right on the lawn in front of Jeff's Jeep, though, so I scooted past the parked cars toward the house.

There were people of all ages everywhere I looked, kids running around the enormous yard, elderly women sitting in the shade of an ancient oak tree. As I walked by the floor-to-ceiling living room window, I could see that inside was just as crowded. Climbing the steps of the deck, I heard my name being called.

"Allison!" Joanne waved at me from one of the French doors leading inside. I smiled and went to say hello. As I approached, she opened the screen door and ushered me inside.

"Hello, sweetheart. I'm so glad you made it. Let me get that for you," she said warmly, taking the salad out of my hands.

I followed her through the mass of people into the

kitchen. She put the salad down on the center island, which was already crowded with similar dishes.

"How's your mom?"

"Pretty good today. The nurse came yesterday to take out her stitches."

"Good. That's good, honey. I really am glad you could come today." Her expression turned mischievous. "Ethan told me you two went to DeeDee's the other night. I always knew he had—"

"What did you always know, Mom?" Ethan appeared from nowhere, poking my side and making me jump.

"Ethan! It's not polite to eavesdrop!" Joanne laughed as she smacked him.

"Hey, now—no hitting!" He rubbed his chest. "And I wasn't eavesdropping, I just wanted to come greet our guest."

"All right, all right. I get the hint," Joanna said. "Have a good time, Allison. I'll talk to you later."

Ethan looked down at me then. His eyes skimmed over my tank top and then back up to my face. "Hey."

"Hey," I mumbled, embarrassed at the smoldering look in his eyes.

That was as much of a greeting as I would get, though, because Nicole and Jeff walked over then.

"There you are, Al!" Nic wrapped me in a hug. "Did you have anything to eat yet?"

"Um, no. I just got here," I said, extricating myself from her grip.

"You've got to try the scallops Jeff's dad is grilling. Oh, and we made these amazing cookies, too. Come on!" She tugged my arm, leading us all out onto the back deck.

As Nicole went on about the food and what I needed to try, I felt the strangest sensation in the back of my head, like someone was tickling my brain with a feather.

Allison…

A enchanting, musical voice, unlike any I'd heard before, whispered my name. I looked around.

Allison, it said again.

I couldn't pinpoint who was speaking. It sounded like it was coming from *inside my head*. But that didn't make any sense…

"I'd just love to try some of your cookies, Jeffrey," I heard Ethan tease. He hadn't heard it, I guess.

"Make fun of me all you want, pal. But, I make some mean peanut butter cookies." Jeff lightly punched Ethan in the shoulder.

Allison…

There it was again. Out of the corner of my eye, I saw two people standing far away from the crowd. *You've got to be kidding.* Liam and a blonde woman I'd never seen before stood close together. I blinked, and they were gone.

Four guys, as tall and as built as Ethan, approached us, each with a beer and a plate of food balanced in their hands. They greeted Ethan and Jeff, and it was obvious they knew each other well.

Ethan stiffened a tiny bit and put his arm around my shoulder. Surprised, I looked up at him.

"Oh, guys. This is Allison, Nicole's cousin. Al, these are the guys on our crew—Ted, Jack, Vinny, and Rich."

I tried to be polite and smile, but my eyes scanned the yard, trying to track down Liam and the mystery woman.

Allison.

The soda can slipped out of my hand and crashed onto the deck, fizzing all over the legs of the men I'd just met. I dropped down onto my knees to grab the offending soda, horrified.

Snippets of past conversations regarding my mother's behavior seeped into my mind.

Aunt Jessie's soft, concerned tone: "*She's always so tense.*"

The deep, baritone of the psychologist: "*It's paranoid schizophrenia.*"

Gram talking quietly with Pop: "*The voices in her head.*"

Hands trembling visibly, I looked up, and my eyes locked on Liam and the blonde, who were across the yard from me. Liam looked uncomfortable; the woman just looked amused.

"Let me just get some napkins," I muttered, searching for anything to clean up the spill.

Ethan frowned at me and followed me to the table that held napkins. "It's okay, Al. It's just a soda, no big deal."

I huffed out a breath, realizing what a fool I was making of myself. I pursed my lips and nodded.

"Hey, where should I put the fireworks?" Sean asked as he and Rachel joined us. I was grateful for their arrival, hoping my embarrassing overreaction would be forgotten. Sean's arm was wrapped loosely around her waist. Apparently they were on-again today. It didn't stop her from batting her eyelashes at the guys, though, and of course, she sneered over at me. Then as if I didn't exist, she turned her back on me and launched into conversation with Nicole.

I tried to relax, listen to the conversations around me, and have a good time. Just before twilight, the guys went out to the fire pit to get the fireworks ready. Nicole and Rachel were at the picnic table near the pool chatting with a group of friends. I saw my chance to take a minute alone so I headed to get another drink.

"This is some party," a familiar voice said from behind me. I turned to see Liam standing in the shadow of the pool house.

"What are you even doing here?" I asked, looking around for the blonde woman he'd been with earlier.

Liam smiled, and his eyes flickered to Ethan. "My new contractor invited me, of course."

"Where is...where is the blonde you were with before?" I ground out. Not exactly the way to convince me he really still loved my mother as he'd claimed.

Liam looked tense and ignored my question. "You have every reason to hate me, Allison. I know that. But I'm here to help your mother, not harm her. There were circumstances that kept me away until now."

"They must have been *some* circumstances."

"I know that's vague." He coughed a little and looked down. "But it's the most I can tell you at the moment."

I laughed, surprised at how cold it sounded. "No comment."

"I know that I'm responsible for your mother's current state. But I really believe I can help her recover."

I twisted to look him in the eye. "I told you I don't want you near her."

"Please, allow me to finish. Helping your mother isn't the only thing I wanted to talk to you about today."

I frowned at him.

"I believe she's in danger."

"My mother is schizophrenic. There is no chance she can, as you say, *recover*." I shook my head in frustration. "And, as far as any danger she might be in, there is *nothing* more dangerous than having her see you again."

"I'm not able to explain further right now, but I'm begging you, please try to trust that I'm telling the truth."

"Trust you? That's a joke, right?" I crossed my arms over my chest.

"We'll be watching to make sure your entire family stays safe," he continued without missing a beat. "But if I do contact you at your grandparents' again, please understand that it's important."

"Wait, what do you mean 'we'?"

Liam looked away, and when he looked back at me, his eyes pleaded with me to understand. Ethan was walking across the lawn, looking from Liam to me with a concerned expression.

"Ethan, your family's home is stunning," Liam said. "Thank you so much for inviting me today, but I'm afraid I must be going."

"All right, man. Talk with you soon." Ethan glanced down at me, a question still in his eyes.

"Allison, lovely to see you again," Liam added with a nod.

I watched him walk away, every muscle in my body thrumming with tension.

"You don't like him much, do you?" Ethan asked, watching me as if gauging my reaction.

"I don't even know him," I replied. Okay, I needed a

change of subject. "Are they almost ready for the fireworks?"

"I think so. Keep your fingers crossed that they know what they're doing."

I laughed at Jeff and Sean across the yard, fighting over a box of matches. Ethan muttered something under his breath, and I turned to see Rachel sauntering over to us.

"Such a great party, Ethan," Rachel sputtered, taking a sip of her wine cooler.

"I'm glad you're having a good time, Rach."

Rachel giggled, batting her heavily made-up lashes at Ethan. "Is it just me, or is it starting to get a bit chilly?"

"I brought a sweatshirt, so I'm fine," I said, pointing to the sweatshirt I'd wrapped around my waist.

"Oh, you're so smart, All-i-son," Rachel stammered. "Do you have a sweatshirt I could borrow, Ethan? I'm getting goose bumps all over." She held her arm up to Ethan's face.

She was such an annoying drunk.

"Yeah, sure. I'll see what I can find," he said, grabbing my hand and pulling me behind him.

"You all right?" he asked, his eyes scanning my face. "You seem upset."

"I'm fine." I tried to smile, but I knew my voice sounded shaky.

"I think I have one of Sean's old sweatshirts up in my room. She can have that," he said as he led me through the house.

"So, are they back together?" I asked him as we walked up the stairs to the second floor.

Ethan snorted. "Sean and Rach? Who knows? Who

cares?"

He paused just inside his bedroom door and turned to look at me. His face was scrunched in concern. "What is it, Al?"

"Nothing. I was just thinking about something Rachel said to my cousin the other day."

He waited for a moment. "Are you going to tell me what it was?" he asked.

"Um, no. I don't think I will," I whispered. I tried to keep my voice from cracking as he moved closer to me.

"Well," he said, his gaze moving down to my lips. "How am I supposed to make you feel better if you don't tell me what upset you?"

I inhaled sharply as he kept moving forward. I took two steps backward before I bumped into the wall.

"She might have said something about you only being interested in me because I'm *no-man's land*," I managed to squeak out.

Ethan chuckled, and I could feel it vibrate through me. "No-man's land, huh?"

"That's right. And she said I'm probably a lesbian, anyway."

His face was inches from mine now.

"You're not a lesbian, are you, Al?" he teased, trying to meet my eyes.

"I don't really have much to base my opinion on," I said, the words just barely audible above the beating of my heart. "I'll have to get back to you on that."

"For the sake of your own peace of mind," he whispered, leaning in so that I could feel his breath on my lips. "I'd be willing to help you figure it out."

My pulse spiked, and I willed it to slow down so that I could form a witty reply. But, he didn't give me a chance. His lips just brushed against mine, soft as a feather. He brought his hands up and cradled the back of my head. *So gentle.* His lips moved against mine—not taking, only asking.

His fingertips trailed down my arm and made me shiver. I pulled back, needing to breath. He didn't let go of me though.

"We should go back outside, before we ruin this by fighting." His smile was genuine, if the slightest bit wistful.

I blushed. Yeah, he was probably right.

Liam walks through a room lit by tiny glowing spheres suspended in the air. The round lights cast shadows on the high-curved walls. He keeps his head bowed as he nears a woman seated on a dais against the far wall. Her hair, as black as a moonless night, is gathered at her neck by a jeweled clip, and hangs in loose waves over one shoulder. Eyes as blue and cold as ice watch him approach.

Liam kneels slowly at her feet, eyes trained on the floor. The woman smiles, and cocks her head to the side like a bird, grabbing his chin and pulling it upward until his eyes meet hers. As he speaks, the woman's face contorts in rage. He winces and she loosens her fingers, leaving behind a bloody trail where her fingernails have cut him. The woman closes her eyes for a moment before shoving him roughly onto his back.

I sat up in my bed, my lungs screaming for air. I pulled my legs up and rested my forehead against my knees as I attempted to catch my breath. Rain beat against my window, matching the drumming of my heart.

For the past six months I'd dreamed about Liam almost every night. Most of the dreams involved blood and fear. They'd gotten more intense now that I'd actually met him too, more foreboding.

The need to go for a run came upon me so suddenly that when I jumped from my bed, my head teetered. I counted backward from twenty as the dizziness subsided and changed into shorts and a tank top. A little rain never hurt anyone.

I inhaled the smell of wet grass as I bound down the front steps. The air was misty, and a gray cloak hung over the trees and early-morning streetlights. It took all of my self-control to force myself to warm-up when all I could think of was launching into a mind-numbing sprint.

The rain eased as I ran, leaving a dreary fog in its wake. After an hour, I looped back around to the bend in the road just before the path to what was now Liam's property.

Allison.

The voice was the same as last night. It made my name sound like a song. But this time there was no one around.

I stopped running, forgetting about cooling down or stretching. My stomach clenched with leftover panic as I looked around in the gloom. I approached the path when Liam stepped out of the trees. His expression was the same uncomfortable one he wore when I saw him last night, as though he dreaded speaking to me.

The blonde materialized next to him, as if the mist had been hiding her body. She cocked her head to one side…reminding me of the woman in my dream. She looked nothing like that raven-haired woman, but she was equally beautiful. Her golden hair was sleek and smooth, cascading down past her shoulders, and her eyes were such a light gray they appeared nearly colorless.

I stopped walking. Something about this woman made me nervous. She smiled at me, her icy eyes glinting, even though the sun hadn't yet made an appearance today.

"Allison," she said out loud in the same voice I'd heard in my head. A shiver raced down my spine when she spoke. Why were they even here?

"Liam? What's going on?" I asked through clenched teeth.

"I wasn't prepared for this," Liam said, his eyes focused on the ground. He was grinding his teeth, too.

"I'm sure you weren't," the blonde said. "But too much time has passed already. You should have known you couldn't put this off forever."

Liam looked at me then, his eyes filled with regret. My heart lurched, and I had the urge to bolt. I shouldn't feel empathy for the man who left my mother pregnant and alone.

"I would've liked to..." He broke off and turned to look at the blonde woman. "She knows nothing of your kind."

Anger and frustration instantly replaced any other emotions that may have been building. "What are you talking about?"

Liam took a deep breath and cleared his throat. "The things I didn't think I could explain to you last night"—he exchanged a look with the woman—"well, it appears I can explain them now."

"Okay," I said, "So, explain."

The woman started walking toward me, her strange diamond eyes holding me captive. "If I may?" It came out as a question, but she didn't appear to actually be asking permission.

"Of course," Liam replied, closing his eyes.

"Your people often use the expression, 'Things aren't always as they appear.'" She paused and I raised my eyebrow, waiting for her to continue. "Whether you believe it or not, your father is here to help your mother."

"Wait." I held my hands up to interrupt. "Who are you?"

She smirked and glanced back at Liam. "My name is Niamh. I am one of the Tuatha de Danaan."

"What?"

"A Danaan—a descendent of the Goddess Danu. You might recognize the term 'fairy' or 'the people under hill'?"

"Fairy," I repeated, the word sounding disjointed from my lips. "Are you a fairy too, Liam?" I choked out a laugh, looking between the two of them. They just stared back at me.

Liam cleared his throat. "Ah, well. I haven't always been..."

"Listen, I don't know what kind of *joke* this is, but my mother is ill. Just stay away from her."

I started to turn around, but Liam held out his hand to stop me.

"Please," he said. "Let me explain."

I threw my hands up in exasperation.

"I was raised in County Monaghan, north of Dublin. I was born the son of a farmer"—he paused and looked me in the eye—"in 1862."

"This just keeps getting better," I said. *Why am I even listening to this?*

"My Da passed away when I was nineteen. I took on many of his responsibilities. After supper I would sneak off to a little clearing in the woods and just play my fiddle until my arms ached."

He stopped and watched for my reaction. I just tapped my foot. "One day as I played, a lovely woman appeared. She told me she had heard the music and wanted to see where it came from. Her name was Aoife, and she was the most glorious creature I had ever seen, with raven hair and eyes like sapphires. I was completely enraptured by her. And the longer I played for her, the more I wanted to make her mine."

Liam paused, his eyes far away, remembering.

"I soon began to long for her day and night. On the days I couldn't slip away, I ached for her—"

"Explain how this has anything to do with my mother," I said. He expected me to believe this?

He ignored my question and continued. "I was becoming physically addicted to her. Aoife and her folk believe that humans are their playthings. They think nothing of capturing a human and filling them with longing, only to dump them back into this world. After their encounters with the Danaan, humans are nothing but empty husks."

Niamh cleared her throat and Liam paused.

"Not all Danaan are so callous," she said. "Aoife is my sister, but we don't share the same beliefs. She has been defying our laws and customs for some time now." She motioned for Liam to go on.

"One day, I begged Aoife to come home with me. She took me to her home instead. By then, I was completely enthralled by Aoife. She was all I cared about. I forgot about my family—they were totally wiped from my mind. And as time went on, I began to come back to myself, my mind began to clear. Just by living in Tír na n'Óg, I was becoming immortal."

"Immortal?" I asked, laughing. "What? Like a vampire?"

"We are as alive as you are, Allison. But unlike your kind, we don't grow old," Niamh said, her lips curving into a smirk.

"So," Liam went on. "I started to remember my life before entering their world. I longed to see my family. I didn't realize that decades had passed here. It seemed such a short time in Tír na n'Óg, because nobody aged there, including me. Aoife would leave occasionally, with only her handmaiden Eithne to watch over me. The first time I asked if I might join Aoife in her travels was in 1979. She agreed to take me along to Dublin.

"Several years later at the Music in the Street Festival at Trinity College, I met your mother."

I thought of the photos I had of Liam and my mother, smiling and happy. Those must have been at the music festival. If any of this were to be believed.

"I couldn't stop thinking about her and planning ways

to see her again. I hid her from Aoife. It wasn't easy, but I had fallen hopelessly in love with your mother. It was nothing like the obsession I'd felt for Aoife—*that* was nothing like love."

Niamh looked away with an uncomfortable expression. When she caught me watching her, I quickly turned back to Liam.

"By then I had become more Danaan than human. I'd stopped aging and had developed some magical ability. Nothing like a true Danaan, but magic nonetheless."

He frowned, and I noticed his eyes beginning to glisten.

"Your mother and I were able to continue seeing each other for about five months before Aoife suspected anything. She assumed I was involved with Eithne, her handmaiden, and began watching me closely. It was nearly impossible to meet with your mother. She didn't understand my situation, and I was too afraid to tell her the truth. I knew I was breaking her heart by staying away, but I didn't have a choice.

"When I returned to Tír na n'Óg, Aoife was waiting for me. She'd figured out with whom I had been meeting and was infuriated I had a desire to be with another, let alone a *human*."

Liam blew out a shaky breath, and Niamh took over. "Aoife's temper is well-known among our folk. But none of us had ever seen such fury as when she felt she was betrayed by Liam," she said shaking her head.

"What did she do to my mother?" I blurted out, anger coloring my tone.

"She didn't do anything to your mother—not directly

anyway," Liam said, his hands balling into fists by his sides. "Aoife placed a geis, an enchantment, on me so that I was unable to touch your mother," his voice faltered. "And then I was forbidden to leave Tír na n'Óg, and your mother left Ireland, thinking I had abandoned her."

I just stared at Liam, though he looked everywhere but at me.

Niamh spoke again, and her face softened. "That's not the worst of it, though. Like Liam said, when humans are abandoned by one of us, they are driven crazy with longing. He experienced it firsthand when Aoife stayed away for just one week. Your mother has been kept from your father for *twenty-two years*. She doesn't have schizophrenia—she has an *unfulfilled addiction*. Until she is able to touch him again, she'll never be more than an empty shell of what she once was."

I felt tears sliding down my cheeks as I listened to Niamh. If this story were true, maybe Liam really could help my mother. For that reason, I wanted it to be true. Another thought hit me hard and fast.

"Where is Aoife now?" I asked, my chest squeezing. "Is she the one who you are trying to protect us from?"

Niamh kept speaking as though she didn't hear me. "During a recent gathering, I sensed something was very wrong with your father."

Niamh looked into my eyes, and I heard her voice in my mind again.

I can read and speak to minds, so I could communicate with Liam without making Aoife suspicious.

"Liam told me everything that happened. I agreed to imprison Aoife in a fey globe. It was the only way to stop her from keeping Liam captive."

Niamh stared into my eyes again. An image of a beautiful woman trapped in a shimmering sphere flashed into my mind.

"Aoife may not be able to cause trouble now, but there are others who would restore her to power—"

"I've seen her," I interrupted. "The black-haired woman in the sphere, I've seen her in my dreams."

I looked at Liam. "When I first met you, I knew who you were because I'd dreamed of you. I knew you were my father because we look...so much alike." I paused for a beat and swallowed hard. *This can't be happening.* "And last night I dreamed of the woman with black hair. *Aoife.*"

Niamh's brow shot up. "I don't understand why my mother didn't tell me about this," she whispered to Liam.

Liam kept his head down. The muscles in his jaw were tense, his hands clenched at his sides.

I couldn't help wondering how her mother would know about me, but my phone rang just as I was about to ask. Ethan's name showed on the display. I turned my back to Liam and Niamh to answer.

"I need your help," he said, sounding distressed.

"Wh-what's wrong?" I asked warily. I didn't know how much more I could handle right then.

"We have way too much leftover food here. Come help me eat it...*please.*"

I let out the breath I had been holding. "Oh, okay," I said, relieved that there was no more earth-shattering news.

"Hey, is everything all right?"

I swallowed the truth, wondering if the fact that my life had just turned into a Disney movie would be considered *all right.*

"Allison," Liam said from behind me in his thick Irish brogue.

"Oh, is someone there with you?" Ethan asked.

"Uh, yeah. I just bumped into Liam while I was out for a run."

"Okay," he said, something off in his voice. "Just give me a call later then."

I put the phone back into my pocket and closed my eyes, trying to reconcile the image of Ethan's face in my mind with everything I'd just heard. What would he think if he knew about all of this?

The answer was simple: he could never know about any of it.

I turned around just as one of the giant black birds landed on a branch just over our heads.

"You have these dreams often, you said?" Liam asked, his eyes darting up to the bird.

I nodded. "Almost every night for about six months."

Niamh's gaze flickered between my father and me as I told them about the dreams. Liam stared at the ground, stroking the back of his neck as I recalled the different scenarios I'd witnessed.

A loud caw came from the trees, and Liam looked up at Niamh, some kind of silent conversation taking place between them.

I put my hands up. "Don't do that. Don't make it so I can't tell what you're saying. Not after all you've put me through already."

Liam cleared his throat. "It was a mistake for us to have met with you out in the open like this."

"It's time for us to go," Niamh said. "It's not safe to stay here any longer."

"So, that's it? You're just going to leave? What am I supposed to do now?" I asked.

"I will see you soon," Liam said, taking one more look at the house where my mother was.

The black bird cawed again and flapped its wings in the tree above.

Go home, Allison.

Niamh and Liam turned as if they were going to walk away, but instead they completely disappeared.

Chapter Six

Monday evening I was at the hardware store closing out the cash register when the bells hanging over the door clanged. I looked up from the receipts to see Ethan strolling up the aisle.

"Oh, hey, Ethan." I looked back down, ignoring the jolt in my heart. I hadn't called him back yesterday after my run-in with Liam and Niamh.

"I was just wondering what time you get off work?"

"Well, as soon as I finish counting up these receipts." I kept my voice casual, keeping my eyes on the papers in front of me.

"Something wrong, Al?" he asked in a low voice.

I shook my head, pretending to be confused. "Not really. I just have a headache."

He shoved his hands in the pockets of his faded blue jeans and shrugged. "You busy tonight?"

"The only thing I'll be doing is taking an aspirin and lying down."

Ethan's mouth tightened, but he nodded.

I wrapped the totals sheet around my receipts and locked them in the safe, avoiding his eyes.

"Everything else is okay though, right? You seem a little...distracted," he said. "And you never called me back..."

"Everything's fine," I said. "Just busy."

I turned off the lights, grabbed my purse, and walked around the counter. He walked by my side to the door, his arm brushing mine as I reached past him to set the alarm. The air felt thick and charged.

Ethan walked me to my car silently. I took a deep breath, and as I turned to face him, a flood of emotions washed through me. Who was I kidding? I'd loved him since before I could remember, reputation and all. But I had a plan: get through school, get a job, and take care of my mother. Being in a relationship was not part of it.

I knew he wouldn't walk away without a fight, but I didn't want to pull him any deeper into my life than he already was. If all of these things with Liam and my mother made no sense to me, how would I ever explain them to Ethan? And if they were true...he'd be in danger. There'd be a rogue fairy out to get me.

"I'll talk to you later, okay?" I said softly.

He was quiet for a minute, and I started getting even more nervous. "I took the day off Wednesday," he said with an odd note of uncertainty. "I wanted to take you to lunch on your birthday."

My mouth went dry, and I realized I'd been holding my breath. I let it out in a puff. "You shouldn't have done that."

Ethan swallowed and looked away, then cleared his

throat. "I'll...I'll just call you Wednesday. Hope you feel better." He tapped the hood of my car before turning and walking away.

Two days dragged by with no word from Liam. I kept replaying the conversation with him and Niamh over and over in my head. They had answers for so many of the questions I'd had my whole life—why I'd never known my father, why my mother lost her mind. And, why I felt like I was losing mine. Their answers sounded *crazy*, but they explained it all so perfectly.

They even acted like my dreams meant something, like I might not be going insane after all. Unless they were just as crazy as I was. Which was highly possible.

I typed the word *Danaan* into the search engine on my laptop, tapping my chin with a pen as I scanned through the results. I'd spent every spare minute the past two days looking up Irish fairies.

The Tuatha Dé Danaan are magical descendants of the pre-Christian deities of Ireland who lived alongside the druids and Gaels. These human-like beings were forced to retreat under the hills of Ireland into another dimension of space and time with the rise of Christianity.

It was reputed that only iron weapons could injure them. They became known as the people of the Sidhe (mounds) or fairies.

Deities? As in gods? I scrolled through web pages on all manner of magic and fairy stories. Paintings of women wearing flowers in their hair with flowing gowns were on every page. *Beautiful.*

I jumped when the phone rang. Again. It had been ringing non-stop all day. I glanced at the caller ID, seeing that it was Nicole this time. I silenced it and tossed it back on my nightstand.

"Allison," Gram called from outside my bedroom door.

I heard the worry in her voice and tried to ignore it. "Come in."

She poked her head in, her brow creased with concern. "Supper's ready, honey." Gram was using her "cheerful voice."

"Okay, I'll be down in a sec," I said as I shut off my laptop.

Gram smiled and tried to make her face look relaxed before nodding and heading back downstairs, leaving my bedroom door open.

The smoky smell of grilled chicken that wafted in from the kitchen made my stomach grumble. I must have forgotten to eat lunch.

Oh my god, lunch!

Ethan had taken the day off so he could take me out for lunch on my birthday. No wonder the phone had been ringing non-stop. I groaned and rubbed my hand over my face. How could I have forgotten? I stood and smoothed my ponytail. I needed to pull myself together for Gram's and Pop's sakes. I was sure they had put together a nice supper while I sulked in my room all day.

I went downstairs, and started when I saw Aunt Jessie and Uncle Dave setting the table.

"Hey, birthday girl!" Aunt Jessie said as she walked by.

Pop came in off the deck carrying a plate of grilled chicken. "There she is! Finally showing her face today. Happy Birthday, young lady!" His eyes twinkled like they always did when the family was all together. As he set the plate down, he kissed my mother on the cheek.

The front door shut with a crash. *Uh oh.* There was only one person missing from the table.

Nicole walked into the kitchen, staring at me with her eyes wide and lips pursed, but said nothing. It might as well have been a slap for what it meant.

Gram saved me by announcing it was time to eat. Everyone loaded up their plates, the typical chatter going on across the table. I was about to take my first bite when Nicole spoke, her voice loud enough to stop all other conversation. "So, Al. I'm glad you're okay."

"I'm fine, Nic," I replied without looking up. I knew my family was looking at Nicole for an explanation.

"That's really good, you know, because I was convinced you were in some sort of accident or that you'd been mugged...seeing that you haven't answered your phone *all* day."

"Nope, I'm all right," I said evenly, fighting the urge to apologize. I had a secret now, something that set me apart from even Nicole, and I had to keep it that way.

"Fabulous." Nicole said sharply.

Gram cleared her throat pointedly, and my head snapped up. My grandparents, aunt, and uncle were quietly cutting the food on their plates, and, my mother was slowly sipping her drink gazing out the back door. Finally, I raised my eyes and met Nicole's hard stare. I shook my head and looked back down at my plate.

I turned on the sink and picked up the sponge. Dinner was over, and helping to clean up was the best excuse I could think of to avoid Nicole. But Gram stopped me.

"It's a beautiful evening, and your birthday, so why don't you go enjoy it on the deck?"

I sighed. It would be no use to argue. I nodded and gave her a kiss, then took my iced tea out back and sat in a lounge chair. Nicole inevitably followed.

She leaned back on the railing and folded her arms. "All right, let's hear it."

"There's nothing to tell."

"I'm used to this sort of thing from you," Nicole began, "but I'm family, I have no choice but to accept your weirdness."

"Nic—"

"No, let me finish. You told Ethan you'd go to lunch with him. Now that I see for myself that there's no catastrophe, I don't understand why you would blow him off."

"First of all, I never agreed. And besides, I haven't been feeling well, and I just laid down for a minute and..." I trailed off, not wanting to lie but hoping Nicole would come to her own conclusions.

"This is Ethan we're talking about, Al. You have been in love with him since you were in the first grade! So, what's the deal?"

"It was a mistake, Nic," I whispered.

Nicole shook her head and stalked back in the house without another word.

I closed my eyes, and let my head fall back on my chair. The sounds of the dishes clattering in the sink began to fade.

I walk into a room. I've seen it before...the curved ceiling is familiar. A man stands in the center of the space, his black hair pulled back at the base of his neck. His face is all sharp angles, and he smirks at me, a cruel and twisted smile. He looks like he's been expecting me, but I've never seen him before.

The cry of bird makes me stop, my feet not wanting to enter any farther into the room. A large black bird lands on the man's outstretched arm, and he looks into the bird's eyes, then back at me.

His laughter is as cold and sharp as an icicle as he turns to look at me again. "Do you know where your mother is, girl?"

"Allie?" I jumped at the sound of my name, and woke to find Ethan gently shaking my shoulder.

"Where is she?" I shouted.

"Whoa, Allie, it's okay. It was just a bad dream," he said as I stood up. "You were kind of thrashing around."

I gulped in the summer air and tried to catch my breath. "I'm...I'm fine. I'm just not feeling that great."

His expression was hopeful. "You must be coming down with something. Nic just told me you slept all afternoon."

I nodded and stretched my arms above my head.

"We were thinking of doing your cake, sweetie," Aunt Jessie said as she stuck her head out the back door and smiled sheepishly at us.

"Oh, thanks Aunt Jessie," I said, grateful for a reason to not have to give Ethan any more explanations. I gave him a halfhearted smile as we headed inside.

My family was seating themselves back at the table with coffee, and in front of my seat was a beautiful cake with lemon icing—my favorite.

As I blew out my candles, I wished for the same thing I did every year—to be strong enough, and capable enough, to take care of my mother.

But, this year's wish was slightly different. I hoped for a real chance at my mother getting better.

When I got up the next morning to go for my run, it was already in the eighties and the sun had barely risen over the trees. The humidity made my tank top stick to my skin, but I didn't care. My headphones blared in my ears, cares shattered into pieces by the pumping bass line. I welcomed the sweat trickling down my back and pushed harder.

I walked the last half mile to cool down, and as I came around the corner I saw Liam standing, once more, in the path leading up to his property.

As I approached, he raised his hand in greeting, and something silver gleamed out from the short sleeve of his shirt.

"Good morning, Allison."

"Hey," I said, feeling awkward and not sure how to act after all he'd told me a few days before.

"They're beginning to clear the property today."

I looked up the path to see a group of men pulling chainsaws out of a truck. "I guess I won't be sleeping in anytime soon."

Liam laughed a little, and his lips curved upward. He had a nice smile—I hadn't seen him smile much since I'd met him.

"I had another dream last night," I said, grabbing my ankle to stretch my leg.

"Oh?"

"Yeah," I said, suddenly unsure if I should share it. He waited for me to continue, and I shook off the fear. "I was in that same room where I saw Aoife before. There was a man with long, black hair. He had a black bird on his shoulder." I looked straight into Liam's eyes. "He asked about my mother."

I didn't like the way his eyes widened at this. "Breanh," he murmured.

"And that means...what?"

"Breanh is Aoife's adviser. He's the one who introduced her to dark magic in the first place. I'm sure he's trying to find Aoife right now."

The way Liam was talking now, fast and without really looking at me, filled me with dread.

"Wait a sec! That doesn't really tell me anything. This guy is the one you think will hurt Mom?"

For a moment, Liam just looked down, his jaw working. When he finally raised his eyes, his expression was tight and reserved.

"If Breanh discovered why I'm here, he'll use your mother against me. In order to get Aoife back."

"I'm guessing letting Aoife go is out of the question?"

Liam sighed. "It would just make everything worse if we released Aoife at this point."

"Worse for who? How can I keep my mother safe if she's now some evil fairy's bargaining chip?"

Liam sighed again, heavier this time. He looked up at the house where my mother was probably watching the early talk shows.

"The workers will keep him away for now, I think. But the nighttime is more of a concern. Stay inside today. I think you'll be safest there."

"No way," I said, raising my voice. "I can't just stay home and hide. I need to do something, find a way to protect her."

"I just need to speak with Niamh, We'll figure something out."

"No, that's not good enough." I was nearly shouting, but the words died in my throat as Ethan's pickup truck pulled up next to me.

Liam turned and walked quickly into the woods in the opposite direction of the workers.

Ethan hopped out of the truck, shutting the door with a *thud*. "Good day for a run," he said with a smile.

"Oh, yeah."

He turned to look at me then. I felt like he could see past all my secrets, so I quickly looked away.

"I just have to go over some things with these guys," he said as he gestured toward the lot next door. "But, after that, I'm free for awhile. You wanna grab lunch?"

"Actually, I was thinking I'd like to spend a little time with my mother before I take over for Lenny at the store."

Ethan nodded slowly, rubbing his hand across his chin. His gaze traveled in the direction where Liam had walked off. "I was hoping to talk to Liam for a minute today, too. Think he'll be back?"

I was caught off guard. "I don't know. He didn't say."

"I had thought..." He struggled to find words, but I already knew what he was going to say.

"What, Ethan?" I asked, keeping my voice low and cool. "You won a *bet*. What more do you want?"

"So, that's it?" He straightened up. "I think we both know it was more than that."

I felt backed into a corner, so, I used the only weapon I had. "I'm sure it's hard for you to believe," I said, adding ice to my voice. "But, it's true."

"Fine." He shoved his hands into his pockets and nodded. "I guess I'll see you around, Al."

He narrowed his eyes and stared hard into mine, stripping me of the last of my defenses. Without another word he turned and walked away.

I headed inside. It really was a scorcher outside. As I headed up the stairs to take a shower I wiped the sweat from my forehead and the tears from my eyes.

Chapter Seven

The hardware store was slow that night, and it was even harder to get through the hours than usual as I was constantly fighting back tears. When I could finally close up, I went straight home. I hadn't heard from Liam yet and it was nearly seven, and between worrying about my mother and replaying my conversation with Ethan, I was completely exhausted and beyond emotionally drained.

Thankfully, everything was quiet when I got home. I walked into the living room to find Gram sitting on the couch folding laundry.

"Just the person I was thinking of," Gram said as I dropped my purse on the sideboard.

"Hi, Gram. Where is everyone?"

"Your mom is upstairs lying down. Pop is down in the cellar, I think."

I sat down in the recliner and leaned my head back for a minute.

"Are you feeling okay, honey? You look a little pale."

I yawned and settled further into the chair, opening one eye to look at her. "Just a little tired, that's all."

Gram stood and hauled the laundry basket up to her hip. "There are leftovers in the fridge, I'm just going to put this laundry away, and I'll heat something up for you."

"I can manage," I said, stretching one more time before I stood.

I took the leftover pasta out and heated a bowl in the microwave. As I waited for it to cook, I sliced a piece of fresh Italian bread.

I wanted to be able to tell Gram everything, to share the weight of all I now knew with someone. But there was no way I could even tell Gram and Pop about who Liam was, let alone all the insane-sounding things he'd told me about his life. Plus, I hadn't had a chance to come to terms with his arrival yet myself, as my father.

I took a deep breath and watched the microwave. Now that my mother was in potential danger, I needed to take care of this myself. There could be no more distractions. But the image of Ethan staring into my eyes, his expression cold and angry, was burnt into my memory. He'd never been angry with me before. But—I reminded myself— angry was better than hopeful.

Once again, I was left waiting to hear from Liam. The hope I'd let myself feel since he'd shown up was being replaced by dread. Liam had said Breanh was dangerous. But would Breanh even know where we were if Liam hadn't shown up here? Now he may as well hand-deliver my mother right to the bad guy.

The ceiling creaked loudly, and I looked up, wondering what Gram was doing up there. It sounded like she was scurrying in and out of the bedrooms. A second later, she bustled down the stairs. Her face was flushed, and strands of white hair escaped from her bun.

The bread knife slipped from my fingers as she approached me, landing with a clatter on the cutting board. Mom. Something was wrong.

"Gram?"

She blinked at me before hurrying over to the living room window. "Your mother isn't in her bedroom," she said as she turned away from the window.

"Tom," she called as she walked toward the cellar stairs and opened the door. "Tom, have you seen Beth?"

"Coming, Jane," I heard Pop holler from the bottom of the stairs. "What is it, dear?"

"I can't find Elizabeth. She isn't down there with you, is she?"

"No," Pop said, wiping sawdust off his brow.

"Maybe she wandered out into the backyard again," I said. Before anyone could respond, I threw open the screen slider and hurried outside. I ran around the entire house shouting her name, but there was no sign of her.

I climbed the porch steps two at a time and charged upstairs to my bedroom. My hands shook as I scrolled through the numbers on my cell phone, trying to find the one Liam had called from.

I heard him pick up but was speaking before he had a chance to say anything. "My mother," I shouted. "She's missing."

After a moment of silence, he finally replied. "I'll be there in just a moment, Allison. Stay put."

I threw the phone down on my bed. Pacing back and

forth, I tried to imagine how this could have happened. How could she have left the house without my grandparents even noticing? It just didn't make sense.

Pop was on the phone when I came back downstairs, and Gram stood by the slider, wringing her hands, looking out into the darkening backyard. My grandfather hung up and walked over to where Gram stood. He wrapped his arm around her, and she leaned her head into his shoulder. I could see she was trembling.

"She can't be far, Jane. I told the police about Beth's condition—they'll be here soon. They'll find her."

"I just don't know how this could have happened," Gram said in a shaky voice.

"Mom?" Aunt Jessie walked down the front hall and froze by the side table, looking back and forth between me and my grandparents.

Gram pulled away from my grandfather and pursed her lips. At Gram's expression, Aunt Jessie rushed over to her.

"She's just...gone," Gram murmured into my aunt's shoulder as they held each other for a moment.

The sound of car doors cut through the tension then, and we were out on the front porch in seconds. A police car was parked in front of the house.

While the officers spoke with my grandparents, I caught sight of Liam standing on the sidewalk a few yards away. He had his back to me, and it wasn't until I was just a few feet from him that he turned around.

"What's happened?" he asked.

I inhaled. "I don't really know. My grandparents thought she was up in her room. But when Gram went to check on her, she wasn't there."

Liam nodded and turned toward the house. His eyes slid over the yard and the vehicles in the driveway.

"You got here so fast," I whispered, barely even aware that I had spoken out loud.

"That's one advantage of being a Danaan." He cleared his throat and glanced over at me. "Speed."

I wasn't sure what that meant, but it wasn't important right now. All that mattered was finding my mom.

I heard one of the officers tell my grandparents that due to her schizophrenia, they'd be able to file a missing persons report immediately. The second officer walked to his squad car to call into the station, while the other continued speaking to Gram and Pop.

Uncle Dave stood at Aunt Jessie's side, rubbing her back as they listened to my grandfather describe my mother's physical appearance.

A car door slammed, and I heard the clatter of heels on tar.

"Al?" Nicole said as she and Jeff walked to the sidewalk. She glanced at Liam and then at me. "Allison? What's going on?"

"My mother," I said, but my voice came out like a croak and I cleared my throat. "My mother's missing."

Nicole's eyes widened in alarm. "Missing? Oh my God." Her arms came up around my shoulders, squeezing me with all her strength.

Jeff spoke from behind Nicole. "Can we form a search party? What are the police doing?"

Nicole didn't give me a chance to answer, she half pulled me toward the rest of our family. I looked over my shoulder at Liam, and he nodded, as though he knew just what to do.

I hurried down the cellar stairs and over to the map of Stoneville that hung above my grandfather's workbench. Standing on my tiptoes, I reached for the pushpins that held it in place. My fingers just barely brushed the rounded heads of the pins, and I strained to get my fingernail underneath. The frantic energy buzzing through my body wouldn't allow me to pop each pin off the board one at a time, and I ended up tearing the map from the wall, barely keeping it in one piece.

I sprinted back to the kitchen and spread the map across the table. My grandparents sat in two chairs pushed close together. Jeff and Nicole, Joanne and her husband Frank, plus half a dozen friends and neighbors had arrived to help look for my mother. Looking down at the street names, I jabbed my finger into the spot that I knew represented our property.

"Okay, we're here. If we divide into groups of four, we can each spread out in all directions..." I looked up to see everyone was waiting for my instructions, as if I really knew what I was doing.

As I assigned paths for everyone to follow, the front door slammed and footsteps came down the hall. Ethan walked into the living room, carrying an armload of flashlights and lanterns. His mouth was set in a grim line and fear flickered in his eyes. I breathed deeply through my nose and looked back down at the map.

I felt each step he took as he came to my side. As I spoke to Ethan's parents and Sean's parent's—the Connor's—I heard the trembling in my own voice.

"You four can take the old cart road up behind the Connor's house. Do you have flashlights?" I grabbed the lantern Ethan held out and passed it to Sean's father, accepting the comfort he offered me with a tight smile.

Allison.

Niamh's voice in my head caused a shudder to ripple across my shoulders. I looked toward the door, but she wasn't anywhere I could see.

Ethan touched my elbow. "It'll be okay, Al. We'll find her."

I looked up to see his brown eyes fixed on mine. He squeezed my arm in reassurance, and I pulled back. I needed to keep my head clear, and his touch was too much.

"Let's go, Ethan. We're going to look behind the old Miller farm," Jeff said as he and Nicole walked over. Nicole's eyebrows pulled down as she assessed the situation.

That's when another familiar voice spoke behind me.

"Mr. and Mrs. O'Malley? I've heard about your daughter," Liam said. "I'll search the woods on the property. She's sure to turn up soon."

My grandparents barely responded, they just gave him watery smiles.

I closed my eyes and sighed. Liam—in my house, talking to my grandparents. About my mother. I had to hold my tongue and remind myself that this wasn't his fault, that he was trying to help bring her home.

I felt Ethan watching my reaction to Liam. I didn't

know what was going through his mind, but I was sure any ideas he had about my relationship with Liam were completely off the mark.

My father turned toward the door. Each assigned search party was making its own plans now, so I followed him out onto the porch. Niamh stood on the sidewalk, and she held me in her gaze as I approached.

Follow me.

I didn't want to, but without hesitating, I followed her to the path leading up to Liam's property. My feet felt like they were moving without my consent.

I gave my word to protect your mother, Allison. No harm will come to her.

I shook my head, not understanding how she could promise that. Or why she would even want to. I got the impression humans meant very little to the Danaans.

I swore to help your father. We will return your mother unharmed.

I sighed. This mind reading thing was already getting annoying.

Niamh smiled wryly. "I can speak aloud if you'd like."

"Thanks," I muttered as we walked farther up the path into the trees.

It was fully dark now, and the moon was waning. The flashlight helped a little, but I still managed to trip over a rock hidden under some leaves. I blew out a frustrated breath and felt someone grab my elbow to steady me. But when I looked over, no one was there.

"Allison, meet Tagdh."

"What?" I asked, looking at Niamh.

"Tagdh is Niamh's guardian," Liam explained. "He's

wearing a glamour to stay hidden from human eyes."

My eyebrows shot up. "What does that even mean?"

"A glamour is an enchantment," Niamh said. "It's like a cloak of magic that keeps your mind from registering his presence."

I rolled my eyes, but nodded as if I heard this kind of thing all the time. "I see."

The air shimmered in front of me, and a young man slowly came into focus. He bowed his head, raising his solemn eyes to meet mine. Their color reminded me of the bright green buds of early spring, and his auburn hair curled around his ears.

"Tagdh was able to use glamour to keep hidden." Liam gestured for me to stop walking now that we were away from the others. "And we have news. The birds we've been seeing around your house are confirmed as Breanh's spies."

Liam watched for my reaction, but I was determined to keep a straight face. "Breanh is able to control the minds of all creatures, including humans."

"Your mother could have easily been coerced to walk right out the front door," Niamh said. "Your grandmother might have seen the whole thing and not remember a bit of it if Breanh wiped her memory."

"So what are we looking for exactly then?"

"Right now, we're keeping up appearances, for your family. Wherever your mother truly is, she's far, far away from here."

Time stopped, and my mouth dropped open. "Keeping up appearances?"

"Your family would think it was strange if you weren't taking part in the search." Niamh shrugged, the slightest pull of her shoulder upward.

"How can you be positive it was Breanh that took my mother? How do you know she didn't just wander off?" I glared at Niamh, but she remained unaffected.

"The chances that she is still in this world are very small," Liam began. "We will go to Tír na n'Óg and see Niamh's mother, Saoirse. She is a Seer, able to see many paths into the future."

I shook my head. "Okay," I said, though I didn't comprehend what that actually meant.

"You will stay here," Niamh added. "Your father and I will go to my mother."

I threw out my hands, breathing hard. "You expect me to sit around and wait?"

"Taking you would be too big of a risk," Liam said.

I gritted my teeth and glared at him. "I need to find my mother."

"I know you're frustrated," he said. "But what's important is that we keep you and your mother safe."

"Obviously our ideas of keeping her safe are very different," I said, spinning on my heel and marching back down the path without sparing another glance at either of them.

I could hear Liam's footsteps behind me as I walked up the sidewalk. I tried to ignore him for as long as possible, but when I stopped he came around to stand in front of me.

"What?" I snapped.

He chuckled a little under his breath as he shook his head. "I've never seen anyone talk to Niamh like that."

I snorted. "Just wait 'til she finds out that I'm going

with you."

"Absolutely not," he said, his posture rigid. "You don't know what you're talking about."

"Don't you see? Niamh doesn't care about my mother—I don't even understand why she's helping you in the first place." I walked around him, heading toward where the crowd still gathered in our front yard. "But if you care about her, you'll take me with you," I called over my shoulder.

Aunt Jessie was talking on the phone when I walked up. I looked around for Gram and saw her surrounded by a group of my mother's old friends, including Joanne. I was grateful that they were there to reassure her.

When Gram saw me, she excused herself from the ladies and hurried over. "Oh sweetheart, how are you holding up?" she asked, placing her palm on my cheek.

"I'm fine. But what about you?"

"I'm terrified, Allie-girl. It's not like your mother to wander off for this long," Gram said, glancing over at Pop.

"We'll find her Gram," I said. I knew Liam could hear me from where he stood on the sidewalk. "I'll do whatever it takes."

My mother lies in a bed, swathed in gauzy fabric, her eyes closed in peaceful sleep. The room is quiet, and warm light comes from globes suspended in the air. A young woman with scarlet hair approaches her bedside, carrying a platter of fruit and a golden cup. Her blue gown looks

straight out of the Middle Ages with floor-length, open sleeves and gilded embroidery on the hems. She bends to place the platter on a table by my mother's head, her hair tumbling over her shoulder.

Another woman with mahogany curls and a similar mauve gown appears on my mother's other side. She laughs as she smooths my mother's hair back onto her silky pillow.

Suddenly, both women straighten up as another walks into the room. Her glistening blonde hair flows to the small of her back. She takes the golden cup in her hands and brings it to her curved mouth. After she takes a sip, she trickles a few drops of liquid onto my mother's lips. As soon as it touches, my mother's eyes open. She stares dreamily at the women surrounding her. She doesn't look afraid—she looks content.

I opened my eyes, and rubbed my palms across my face before looking at the clock.

4:43 a.m.

I must have fallen asleep on the couch while waiting to hear from the police.

It took a minute to clear the cobwebs from my head. I could still almost smell the ripe fruit and hear the laughter from my dream. I reached over and patted the end table until I found my cell phone. I clicked it open and tapped a text message to Liam:

Where are you?

Not ten seconds later, my phone beeped with a message:

Right outside.

My eyebrows furrowed. Had he really waited for me?

I stood and walked to the window that looked out on the woods next to the house. A sliver of the moon still hung low in the sky, but it was too dark to see anything.

I sent another message:

What are you still doing here?

After a brief pause, my phone beeped again:

Niamh went without me.

I looked up from my phone and out into the trees. I squinted and saw a tiny bit of movement in the woods. Slipping on my flip flops, I hurried out the sliding door. The sky was streaked with the lavender and peach light of early morning as I walked toward the spot I'd seen the movement.

"Good morning."

I jumped as Liam appeared out of nowhere beside me. "How did you do that?"

He chuckled, the sound so quiet I barely heard it. "I told you—we're fast. Too fast for you to see."

I closed my eyes and inhaled. *Nothing should surprise me anymore.*

"Why didn't you go with Niamh? And why are you standing in the woods at this hour?" I asked, glancing up at him.

He looked toward the sky as he rubbed the back of his neck. "It didn't feel right," he began, his accent thick. "Leaving you here didn't feel right."

My eyes widened and I swallowed hard to hold back the biting comment that came to mind. "What about my mother?"

"Allison, this is all happening so fast and I know

you're frustrated." He swallowed, shooting me a pleading look.

"You worried about what I might do, didn't you?" I said, the realization striking me as I spoke.

He cleared his throat and shrugged. "You're the first daughter I've ever had," he said.

I rolled my eyes. "All right, fine. Does this mean you're taking me to fairy land?"

Liam sighed. "I suppose it does."

The screen door bounced a few times before it shut behind me as I walked back into the house. I smelled coffee brewing and heard dishes clanking in the sink. As I passed the den, I saw my mother's violin sitting in its case, open on the coffee table. It looked like she had just been about to take it out before she'd disappeared, not up in her room at all.

Gram sat at the table, idly stirring a cup of coffee in front of her, while Pop gazed out the back window. Aunt Jessie stepped away from the sink where she was washing the dishes from the night before.

"You all couldn't sleep either, I guess…. Any news?" I asked, as they all looked at me questioningly.

Aunt Jessie smoothed back my hair and smiled at me with pity in her eyes. "No, honey. Nothing yet. There were a couple calls during the night but"—she sighed—"they were all dead ends."

It was all I could do to keep my mouth shut. I wanted

to tell them they were all wasting their time, that I was going to find her and bring her home myself.

"I'm just going to grab some breakfast, and I'll be heading back out," I said instead.

Uncle David walked into the room holding up his phone. "Nic said she'll come here first, and you can go out with them. They're about to head to the mall to see if for some reason she wandered down there."

I shook my head. "I'd rather split up for now, cover more ground."

Pop cleared his throat, and when I looked over at him I froze. His face was ashen, with dark circles shadowing his eyes. "Allie, please don't go out alone. Wait for your cousin."

I felt a sharp twang of guilt as I packed my duffel bag. Leaving might hurt my grandparents a little at first, but it would be worth it when I brought my mother back safely. Staying here to keep them calm now would be worse in the end. As I zipped my bag closed, my bedroom door opened slowly.

Nicole stuck her head in, her expression worried. "You planning a trip, Al?"

"Actually...yes. And you're just in time to help me."

Nicole frowned. "I don't think I like where this is going."

"Come on, I never ask you for anything. I need you to cover for me, to keep Gram and Pop from worrying," I said as I picked up my bag. "Now, I can't tell you where I'm going, but you need to just trust me."

"Are you kidding? You're just leaving, and you expect me to cover for you without *any* information. Of all the times for you to lose your cool, Al."

I put my hands on Nicole's shoulders and looked directly into her eyes. "I need you now, more than I have ever needed anything. I am going to find my mother, and you need to have faith in me. Whatever you have to say, just cover for me."

Shaking her head, Nicole turned away. "Fine, but don't do anything stupid. It's not like you to be so crazy. *Please* don't do anything stupid," she repeated

"Thanks, Nic…really."

"Did I mention I don't like how you're acting?" Nicole said over her shoulder, walking out of my bedroom.

I met Liam in the clearing after I snagged a few snacks to bring with me. He looked curiously at the bag slung over my shoulder.

"You're ready, then?"

"Yep, I'm ready."

"And you're sure about this?"

"Stop stalling. How are we getting there?"

"The portal is at Niamh's house, about an hour from here." he said, hesitating. "By car. But if we run, we'll be there in about a minute."

My eyebrows shot up and I gasped.

"I know, I know. But it's true."

I shook my head. "Maybe you can run at light speed, but I can't."

"Allison," he said, as if I was being ridiculous. "I'll carry you."

"Whoa, I don't think so. I'd rather drive."

"We're wasting time," he said, his jaw tightening. "It'll be over very fast. You won't even have a chance to think about it."

I looked at him a moment longer. "Fine." I threw my hands out. "Carry me."

In a flash, he had me up over his shoulder like a fireman rescuing a child, and the air was sucked straight out of my lungs like a vacuum. The change from standing still to flying through the air was so intense that I swore I left my vital organs in the wooded lot. I tried to pry open my eyelids, but the pressure kept them locked down. The only thought I had was of falling from Liam's shoulder and exploding into a million pieces.

When Liam slowed down and I felt the pressure release, my lungs automatically gulped in air. I opened my eyes to see grass and boulders and a dirt road blurring by. Then he came to a complete stop and I wriggled off his back. My equilibrium was still in Stoneville, so I was glad he held me steady by the elbows. I might have gone down like a sack of rocks otherwise.

The trees on either side of the road towered above us, their long branches intertwining overhead to give the impression of a tunnel. The grass was wild and tall around the two indents of the road. It was obvious that no vehicles had been up this way in quite some time.

"Niamh's house is just around that bend," Liam said, walking along the overgrown path.

I followed closely behind, keeping underneath the green canopy where the air was cooler. The only sounds were the chirping of songbirds and our footsteps on the earth.

"It's pretty here. But why are we in the middle of the woods?"

"We're backed up to a wildlife preserve in Wheelwright. We try to stay away from iron as much as possible, so this spot is perfect."

"How can you stand being in Stoneville then? Iron and steel are everywhere."

"We use magic," he said, glancing at me sideways as he walked. "There is no iron in Tír na n'Óg, as you can imagine. There *is* a mineral known as fháillan, however. Fháillan is, in many ways, the opposite of iron."

He lifted the sleeve of his shirt. A silver-colored band decorated with intricate swirls and triskelions encircled his upper bicep. *That's what I must've seen those days ago.*

"This fháillan band repels the effects of iron for a time. It's not complete, but it's bearable."

As we walked, I thought about the dream I'd had the night before. "I dreamed of my mother last night."

"Oh?" he asked, waiting for me to continue.

"She was in a room, surrounded by these women. One of them was so beautiful it practically hurt to look at her. They were all smiling and laughing."

Liam's eyebrow furrowed. After a moment, he asked, "What did the woman, the one you said was beautiful, what did she look like?"

"She had long, pale blonde hair. Her skin was equally pale, flawless. At first I thought it was Niamh, but Niamh's hair is much more golden."

"That sounds like it might be Niamh's mother, Saoirse," Liam didn't seem to actually be talking to me, but rather thinking out loud.

"I hope that's a good sign, that my mother seemed happy."

Liam didn't say anything, just kept walking until we came to a vast clearing. The rolling hills were dotted with purple and yellow wildflowers. Nestled between two ancient oak trees sat a pale blue shaker-style farmhouse. It appeared to be at least two hundred years old, yet impeccably maintained.

As we opened the front doors, we heard low voices. I widened my eyes as Liam gestured for me to follow him inside.

The old wooden floorboards creaked under our feet, and the house smelled of wood and old, oiled leather. In the small foyer, a staircase led to a second floor. Doorways were at both sides of the room.

Sitting at a round wooden table to the left were two young men, one I recognized as Tagdh. He didn't seem very surprised to see us, though. He smiled tightly and glanced across at a man with shaggy black hair. It seemed as though they were expecting us, even.

A large map lay on the table in front of them. I didn't recognize the locations, but there were little blue beads dotted over its surface.

The black-haired man rose to his feet. "Liam. We were wondering when you'd arrive." He spoke with a thick Irish accent. His gazed moved past Liam to rest on me.

"Allison, meet Diarmuid, Niamh's advisor," Liam said.

Diarmuid looked at me curiously. His eyes were soft blue and gentle. "Lovely to meet you, Allison."

"And, you met Tagdh in Stoneville," Liam said.

Tagdh stood and inclined his head and looked at me with a blank expression. I tried to smile at them, but it came out more like a grimace.

"Liam." I turned to see a young woman with wavy, ginger hair come through a swinging door.

She hurried to place the plate of fruit she was carrying on the table and turned to Liam. She grabbed his arms, and her gaze ran up and down the length of him.

"I'd heard you were all right, but I'm so glad to see for myself." She turned to me, confusion plain on her face. "And, who's this?"

The woman released Liam and tilted her head to the side as she appraised me. I felt heat creep up my neck.

Diarmuid came to stand at the woman's side. "This is Allison. Liam's daughter."

"Daughter?" The woman stood frozen, looking at Liam with utter shock.

Liam cleared his throat. "It was a surprise for me as well."

For an awkward moment there was only silence.

"Forgive me, Allison. I'm Eithne. Come, sit." Without meeting my eyes, she gestured to a chair across the table, and I sat down. Liam took the chair next to mine.

"Eithne was once Aoife's handmaiden, the one I told you about," Liam said. "She and Diarmuid are bond-mates, similar to a married couple."

Liam waved his hand at the map, clearly done explaining. "I'm guessing Aodhan is on another mission?"

Diarmuid leaned back in his chair. "That he is."

Now, that I was closer, I could see that the map showed the Northern United States and Canada, most of the beads concentrated in lower Ontario.

"Who's Aodhan?" I asked. "Does he have something to do with my mother?"

Eithne's eyebrows shot up and her mouth formed an O.

"Aodhan, like your father, was once human," Diarmuid said.

The other three Danaans kept their eyes cast on the floor, and I got the impression that talking about Aodhan made them uncomfortable for some reason.

"After a time in our realm, he wished to visit his family. When he returned, they were long gone. He'd been in Tír na n'Óg nearly three hundred years, but now he lives here, alone, hunting for Danaans who harm humans."

I wished we had someone like him on our side. He sounded like just the guy to help get my mother back from Breanh.

"My brother Niall tracked him to Canada," Tagdh continued. "There are reports of serial killings up in Thunder Bay. Humans left completely drained of blood just left on the streets." Tagdh's voice was strangely void of emotion considering the gruesome news he shared.

"Is there a portal there that's been left unguarded?" Liam asked.

Eithne got up and excused herself, exchanging a look with Diarmuid. *Huh. What was her deal?*

"There's one just over the Canadian border. Since Aoife was imprisoned, her folk have been running wild up there. It was just a matter of time before Aodhan caught up with them."

Liam cleared his throat and turned away, but I could see his jaw clench. Between his reaction and Eithne's I guessed there was more to this story than I was getting.

"Does Niamh know about the situation up there?" Liam asked, still gazing out the window.

"No, when she first came here, her father showed up in a rage. She went back to Tír na n'Óg before we had a chance to tell her," Diarmuid said.

Liam's head swiveled in Diarmuid's direction. "Deaghlan was here? Does he know what's happened with Aoife?"

Diarmuid and Tagdh both hesitated.

"He does, Liam. Breanh told the King and Queen everything."

Liam smacked his palm on the table and muttered an oath under his breath. "Where is the fey globe now?"

"Deaghlan demanded that Niamh give it to him."

Liam swore, louder this time. "We need to go, Allison. Deaghlan is Aoife and Niamh's father. If he releases Aoife, she'll go back to Breanh. Things could go very wrong if we don't hurry."

Butterflies as big as helicopters filled my stomach. "Why would Deaghlan let Aoife out?" I stammered. "What about all the trouble she's caused?"

The muscles in Liam's jaw popped under his skin. "Deaghlan doesn't value human life. Humans are just playthings at his disposal. I'm fairly certain he doesn't even think Aoife has done anything wrong."

I stared at Liam for a moment. It was like a nightmare, where no matter what you did things just got worse. How could I have lived my entire life without knowing these people existed? And now they held everything I cared about in the palms of their hands.

"If Breanh has my mother, and Aoife goes there..." I couldn't even finish that sentence.

"Liam?" Diarmuid asked. "What will you do?"

"We're going to Tír na n'Óg to get Allison's mother before something terrible happens to her."

Diarmuid and Tagdh rose gracefully from their seats. "We've been given specific orders not to allow you to enter the portal."

"I don't understand," Liam said, looking between the two men. Both stared back blankly.

My heart plummeted at their grave expressions, and I knew that we would not get past them without a fight. They were stronger and faster, and who knew what kind of magic they were capable of. It wouldn't be a fair fight. And judging by Liam's frown, he knew it, too.

I stared down at the table, running my finger along the image of the Great Lakes. Why would Niamh forbid Liam to go through the portal? I'd been wary of her before, but I didn't think she would purposely keep Liam from being able to help find my mother.

"Maybe it's best this way," I said, pushing up from the table.

At any other moment, I'd have paid money to see the incredulous look on Liam's face. But the beginning of a plan had taken root in my mind. And in order for it to work we needed to hurry.

I stood up and walked straight out the door without another word.

Chapter Eight

I counted my steps as I walked away from Niamh's house. Frustration and panic boiled inside me, but I needed to keep calm. I stopped walking when I realized Liam wasn't with me.

I was *not* going back in there. The Danaans were lovely to look at, but their behavior was not normal. It was as if they were made of stone, incapable of emotion.

Minutes passed and Liam still hadn't come out. I paced back and forth in the field, willing myself not to panic. When the front door slammed, I turned to see my father at my side in an instant, his expression wary.

"You're taking all of this too well," he said, his brow furrowed.

I sighed, knowing this would be a fight. "I've come up with a plan."

He stiffened. "Oh?"

"You and I are going to go find this Aodhan guy and bring him back here," I said, nodding toward the house. "I can tell those two are at least a little afraid of him. We need someone on our side."

"Absolutely not," he said.

"Niamh doesn't care about my mother," I said. "Who knows what she's doing now? If you want to find my mom, you'll come with me to ask this guy for help. Otherwise, I'll go alone."

"You've only seen a handful of the Danaans, Allison. You don't understand what you're dealing with. Did you hear what Tagdh said in there? *They're draining the blood of humans.* Aoife's folk are involved in all sorts of forbidden magic."

"All I care about is getting my mother home safely. Are we supposed to just sit around until Niamh comes back before we do anything?" I put a hand on my hip, acting braver than I felt. "I get that Breanh isn't someone I can face on my own. But maybe Aodhan will help us." I paused. "I have to do something, and if this is all I can do, I've got to try."

Liam looked away from me, past the trees to the hills in the north. After a few minutes, he exhaled and looked back at me.

"I suppose you're right. We need to do something and waiting on the whims of Niamh is not looking like much of a plan now."

"I'm ready. Are we going to...*run* again?"

"I guess that was more uncomfortable for you than I expected." He took a couple steps toward me, put his hands on my shoulders, and looked into my eyes. I stared back, and then everything went black.

A young woman with fire-truck red curls and multiple facial piercings clings tightly to a guy's arm as they walk through a large, mirrored door. The guy is tall with black gelled spikes and tattoo-covered arms. She scans the darkness surrounding them while they walk toward an alley. He looks pleased at the way she is pressed tightly to his side.

"Tori, look, there's nothing there. It's okay."

The woman pouts her full, black-painted lips and buries her face in his arm, making a low whimpering sound.

"Seriously, how many of those drinks were for you, and how many did you give Val?" he asks her, laughing.

"I'm not that drunk, Wes. I'm telling you I heard something." She pulls away from him and smacks his arm before the heel of her black boot catches on a crack on the sidewalk, making her stumble. The guy kneels by her side as she examines the tear in her black fishnet stockings.

Without either of them noticing, two tall shapes move out of the shadow of a striped awning, heading straight toward them.

"Allison." My eyelids fluttered open to Liam staring down at me in concern.

I took a deep breath and blinked, trying to figure out where I was. I lay in the center of a double bed, in an unfamiliar room. *A motel room?*

The walls were dingy white and the bedspread smelled

like fabric refresher—chemicals covering unwanted body odor. There was one large window with its floral drape pulled closed. On the bedside table, a tiny lamp cast shadows on the wall, and the alarm clock flashed 12:00 in red.

"We're in a motel in Thunder Bay," Liam said. He was sitting on the side of my bed, looking down at me.

I sat up and stretched my arms over my head and yawned. "Did you cast a spell on me?" I asked, moving my fingers and toes, feeling a little groggy.

"No, not exactly. Mind magic doesn't really work like that. I was able to coerce you to go to sleep."

"All right," I said slowly as I stood up. A horrible possibility occurred to me. "You could coerce me to do whatever you wanted?"

He looked aghast. "I suppose I could, Allison, but I wouldn't. I still have my humanity."

I glanced at him out of the corner of my eye. Did he? I sure hoped so.

"Before we left, though, I found out a little more about the situation up here," Liam said, changing the subject.

I raised my eyebrows as I waited for him to continue.

"Aodhan is staying at a motel adjacent to a nearby crime scene." He pulled a slip of paper out of his pocket and glanced up at me before continuing.

"The entire area is on alert because of a suspected serial killer. There was a group of teenagers murdered on their way home from a concert Wednesday night. Then on Friday, a bartender and his girlfriend were found completely drained of blood not far from the spot where the teenagers' bodies had been discovered."

I sucked in a breath. "That's *awful*." The memory of the dream I'd had of the couple out walking played in my mind.

"Yes. What they're doing, this kind of magic, it *taints* them. Makes them wicked. And they don't give a damn if they leave a mess behind."

"What do they actually use the blood for?" I asked, not positive I wanted to know the answer.

"There are two kinds of magic the Danaans can use. One is mind magic. It is all about being able to control things with ones will. For instance, Eithne is a healer. She is able to use her mind to see what it is that ails you and reverse it. Niamh is able to use her mind to hear your thoughts and share hers.

"The other is elemental magic. It involves using outside forces. Some aspects aren't bad, but what it sounds like Aoife's guards are doing has been forbidden by Saoirse for a very long time. They're taking the blood of humans and harvesting the small levels of magic in it to increase their own abilities."

"So humans have magic in them too?"

"That's right."

"Did Diarmuid and Tagdh tell you all this?"

"After you walked out they told me that Tagdh's brother, Niall, is one of the guards tracking Aodhan."

I nodded and went to get a cup of water from the tap. I took a sip and then glanced at myself in the mirror hanging by the bathroom. My hair was a disaster, and I had circles rimming my eyes. No surprise there.

Once I pulled myself together, Liam took out his cell phone and opened the door. I watched him curiously but kept quiet as I followed him outside.

The motel was like the dozens of others I'd seen in my life, with the lot butted up to a highway. We walked out to the sidewalk, and I looked around. Thunder Bay was a busy place. Cars were flying past and people rushed around, talking on cell phones or yelling to their friends. Across the street was a park littered with people playing Frisbee or walking their dogs. Beyond the park, I could see a marina that edged out into Lake Superior.

Liam's phone snapped shut, and I looked over at him. "That was Niall. He's about three blocks away. Let's go."

We walked past several businesses and apartment buildings until we came to a corner where one of the murders had taken place. Two buildings down, on the side-street, were three metal doors with mirrors on their surfaces. I looked at the reflective doors, and my jaw went slack.

The doors from the dream I'd had on our way to Thunder Bay.

A black sign above the door read *Black Pirates Pub* in curling, white letters.

Liam stopped walking, not noticing my preoccupation. His lips curved into a little smile. Following his gaze to a bench, I saw a man with shoulder-length chestnut hair reading a newspaper. He put the paper down and turned. As soon as he recognized Liam, the man stood and walked over to greet us.

"Liam," he said, clapping him on the shoulder and glancing curiously at me.

"Allison, this is Niall. Without his help I may have never escaped Aoife in the first place."

Niall smiled, clearly glad to see my father. "So, Liam, what news do you bring?"

"I'm afraid I don't bring good news. We've come to find Aodhan to seek aid."

"Good luck there, my friend," Niall laughed.

Liam made a face. "We must at least try."

"Have you found your lady, then?" Niall asked, looking at me.

Liam cleared his throat. "Yes, but this is actually my...daughter." The corner of his mouth lifted.

Niall pursed his lips, as if trying not to laugh. "Indeed."

"Have you seen Aodhan today?" I asked, pushing down my embarrassment at Niall's amused expression. We were running out of time.

Niall shook his head, still surveying me. "He usually stays inside during the day. He'll be coming out once it gets dark. Give him a couple hours."

"This is the pub where the couple had last been seen Friday night," Liam cut in, looking up at the sign.

"Yeah, I know," I nodded.

Liam's eyebrow quirked up. "Did you just say 'I know'?"

"Well, yes. I had a dream about a couple walking out of there," I said, gesturing toward the doors to the pub. I looked back at Niall as I walked toward the three metal doors at the entrance.

"Blá's watching the back exit. We'll let you know when he comes out." Niall said as he sat back down on the bench.

"Blá?" I asked Liam.

"Bláithín is Niall's partner. There are always at least two guards assigned to watch Aodhan," Liam said with a sardonic grin.

I paused before opening the door. "What?" I asked.

Niall now wore the same wry expression as Liam. "Nothing," he said, trying to hide his grin. "It's just that Niamh wouldn't risk losing track of Aodhan."

I huffed in exasperation. "If Aodhan isn't out yet, we should get something to eat, maybe ask a few questions—let's go."

Inside, the Black Pirate was quiet. There were a few employees setting up tables, and at the end of the long, polished bar was an easel holding a blown-up photo. I recognized them as the couple from my dream. A wreath of flowers hung on the corner, and several teddy bears and bouquets were placed nearby.

Liam and I sat at the far end of the bar. As we opened our menus, a man with a white button-down shirt approached from the other side of the mahogany.

"Good afternoon. My name's Jack. What can I do for you?"

"I'll just have a BLT," I said, picking the first thing I saw on the menu. Liam ordered the same.

"Are you two here on vacation, or just passing through?" Jack asked as he took our menus.

"We're just passing through, actually. Seems like a rough time around here, eh?" Liam said, gesturing to the easel by the bar.

Jack's face fell. "Oh, yeah. Such a tragedy. Wes was the bartender here a couple nights a week."

"Wow. What *really* happened?" Liam asked, looking hard into Jack's eyes.

"They're saying serial killer. Must be a real psycho," Jack said, launching into the story of all the bodies being found drained, six altogether.

After we ate, we walked back outside, and Niall was gone.

"I guess Aodhan's on the move."

Liam opened his phone and typed a message. We sat on the bench and waited for Niall to respond.

Minutes passed and still nothing.

"Can we take a walk down to the water, just to look around?" I said, itching to do something.

Liam looked at me for a couple seconds, considering. "Right, let's do that."

We crossed over to the park and down to the marina. A light breeze blew off Lake Superior, rustling the leaves above our heads as we walked down the path. The only other sound was the occasional faint whir of traffic up on the street.

Liam walked close by my side, his eyes constantly roaming the area.

"I feel like there's something you're not telling me about Aodhan," I said.

Liam coughed, looking uncomfortable. "The situation with Aodhan is...complicated."

"Did you know him?"

"I knew him briefly. When I first arrived in Tír na

n'Óg, he had just started asking about his family. He'd been there the equivalent of nearly three hundred years and had *no idea.* The time passes differently there, especially when you're in thrall."

"In thrall?" I interrupted.

"Well, yes. Aoife had me so deeply under her spell, I had no will of my own. All that mattered was her."

"Oh, okay. Go on."

He sighed but continued. "When I met him, he asked me about the war. As I told him, he looked at me like I was daft. The Ireland of 1602 was a far cry from the Ireland of 1888, I'm sure you can imagine."

The park was deserted, only the long shadows of the oak trees crisscrossed the path in front of us. "We should head back, see if we can find Niall."

I inhaled and we turned back up toward the street. "I wonder if—"

Before I had the chance to finish, a shadow moved ahead of us.

"Liam," a tall figure said, pushing away from a tree just five yards away.

I froze on the path as the man walked down to where we stood. As he got closer, I took in his gaunt features and sunken eyes filled with malevolence.

"Stay back," Liam hissed, pushing past me.

"Has Aoife let you off of your leash?" the stranger asked.

Something shifted in Liam's stance, he stood straighter and tension rippled through his body.

"This is all your doing, Aengus?" Liam gestured to the city.

"How long is your mistress going to keep us locked out of Tír na n'Óg?" Aengus asked, ignoring Liam's question.

"I don't know anything about you being locked out. Things have been"—Liam hesitated—"out of sorts in Tír na n'Óg. You can probably thank Breanh for keeping you out."

Liam looked back at me, but quickly realized his mistake when Aengus noticed me standing there. Before I could even try to move, Aengus appeared in front of me. He reached out and stroked my jaw with a long, bony finger.

"Ahh, and who do we have here?" he asked, his warm breath blowing in my face as his eyes raked over my skin.

Liam ran back to my side and grabbed Aengus's hand to shove him away. I heard the metallic whoosh of a blade, and in a flash, Liam was on his knees. The color drained from his face, and I looked down to see the handle of a knife sticking out of Liam's side.

Before Aengus's sneer had a chance to fully form, he was knocked to the ground by a blur of silver light. I quickly figured out that the silver blur was actually a gigantic man, dressed all in black with a closely-shaved head.

Without hesitation, the man yanked Aengus's head back by his hair and put a wicked-looking dagger to his throat. Aengus grimaced as the edge of the dagger drew a thin line across his neck.

I rushed to Liam's side as his body went limp, and I struggled to get him down to the ground without injuring him more. He tried to speak but all he could manage was a low gurgling sound.

"Shhh," I crooned, trying to calm him. I sat him in an upright position as I scrambled to figure out how to help him. I needed to put pressure on the wound, but the dagger was still sticking out. And I knew that if I pulled it out, it would increase the blood flow.

"Aodhan," I heard Aengus hiss between clenched teeth. "Another pleasant surprise."

"You like torturing the innocent, do you?" Aodhan asked as he yanked Aengus's head back further.

"Just kill me and get it over with," Aengus spat.

"Oh, no. That would be much too easy," Aodhan growled as he pulled a cord out of his pocket, the dagger still held firmly to Aengus's throat. "How do *you* like being tortured?"

Aodhan secured Aengus's hands behind his back and lifted a length of steel chain from a cargo pocket at this thigh. He put the dagger between his teeth and wrapped the chain around Aengus's throat.

Aengus groaned, and his knees buckled out from under him. Aodhan shoved him to the ground and looked up at me. I could only stare back in silence. There was something familiar about this guy.

His gaze flickered over my shoulder. "Take care of him," he snarled.

I looked back and saw Niall approaching cautiously. His eyes remained on the sprawled form of Aengus lying face down on the pavement. Without a word, Aodhan approached us and gently lifted Liam up.

"Come on," Aodhan said to me, his Irish accent thicker and harder to understand than Liam's. "We need to take care of his wound."

I nodded and followed Aodhan up the deserted street toward his motel. The bartender had told us the city had imposed a curfew, and there wasn't a soul out now that dusk had fallen.

Aodhan's room was on the second floor, but he carried Liam up the flight with no trouble at all. He pulled out a key card and unlocked the door, pushing it open and laying Liam on the bed.

Relief flooded through me that he wasn't bleeding as much as I'd feared, but his shirt was ruined.

"Get the towels from the bathroom and fill the basin with hot water," Aodhan instructed.

When I came back with the supplies, he had Liam's shirt off, and I could see that the dagger stuck just below his rib cage on his left side. His milky-white skin was covered in a sheen of sweat and streaked with a rivulet of blood.

"I'm going to pull this out. When I do, I want you to immediately apply the towel to the wound."

I unfolded the towel and knelt by Liam's side. His eyes were closed, and his breathing was shallow.

"Ready?" Aodhan said.

I nodded.

The blade made a wet, squishy sound as he pulled it out in one swift movement.

"Now."

I applied the towel, holding the gaping wound together with as much pressure as I could.

"Good, it will only take a few minutes for the bleeding to stop. It's not as bad as I thought."

He walked over to the chair by the window and opened a duffel bag. Inside was a small first-aid kit.

"Should we get him to a hospital?" I asked, biting my lip.

Aodhan leveled me with his gunmetal eyes. "No, he's just unconscious. His body is trying to heal itself."

He walked to the window, opening the heavy drape just a crack. The muscles in his jaw were tense as he scanned the night.

"Aodhan—" I began.

Aodhan held up his hand, effectively silencing me. He turned away from the window, eyeing both me and my father thoughtfully. His gaze rested on Liam.

"I knew I recognized him…Aoife's pet."

I didn't know how to respond to that, but Aodhan wasn't done.

"I've grown accustomed to Niamh's minions following me all these years. But," he said narrowing his eyes, "for the life of me, I can't imagine what Liam would want from me."

The way he spoke, so low and empty of emotion, filled me with cold fear. I could feel my heart pounding in the tips of my toes, like flames licking at ice.

"It was me who wanted to find you," I said, my voice taut.

He slowly turned to me, and it was all I could do to keep from shrinking back. "What is it *you* want from me?"

I closed my eyes and scrounged for every shred of courage I could find. "My name is Allison, I'm Liam's daughter," I began.

"My mother was kidnapped by Breanh. I was hoping

you could…could," I stuttered. " I was hoping you could help me get her back."

"*Breanh,*" Aodhan said, but it came out as a low growl.

"Liam has Aoife imprisoned in a fey globe." I stole a glance at Liam before launching into the full story.

Aodhan leaned against the wall as I spoke, not interrupting, only nodding occasionally. I told him about Niamh and Liam showing up in Stoneville and the black birds that were everywhere, always watching. I told him about the night my mother had gone missing and that Niamh had gone back to Tír na n'Óg without us, effectively shutting us out. I even told him about the dreams I'd been having for months. There was something trustworthy about him.

When I finished talking, Aodhan straightened and walked to the tiny table in the corner of the room. In one fluid motion, he pulled the dagger he'd held to Aengus's throat from its sheath on his hip. Then, from a wooden box, he pulled a small square of red cloth with which he began to wipe the dagger.

Without turning around, Aodhan spoke, his words clipped. "Do you know where he's taken her?"

"We're assuming he's taken her to Aoife's home in Tír na n'Óg."

There was a knock at the door, and for a second Aodhan just stared at it. He walked over to open it. Niall stood there with a tall, black-haired woman I assumed was Bláithín, his partner. His eyes flickered in to me and then Liam before resting on Aodhan's massive chest.

"We wanted to see if Liam was okay," Bláithín asked,

running her fingers through her short, spiky hair. She, unlike Niall, obviously had no problem meeting Aodhan's fierce look.

Aodhan stepped aside, and let them into the motel room. Bláithín hurried over to the bed and placed her hand on Liam's cheek.

"Where's Aengus's dagger?" she asked, looking between Aodhan and me.

"There on the floor, just under the bed," I whispered. Aodhan had gone back to leaning against the wall, clearly uncomfortable with all the company.

"This dagger is steel, just like I thought," she said, toeing it with her boot. "It looks like the tip is broken off, too."

"Come on, Allison," Niall said. "We'll take you and your father back to Niamh's house in Wheelwright. He needs to see a healer to get the tip of the dagger out. Hopefully Eithne is still there."

All three Danaans looked at me expectantly. If I went with Niamh's guards, I'd be expected to wait on Niamh's whim. I needed Aodhan to come, too.

I looked at him, silently praying. He hadn't agreed to help yet.

He met my gaze. "I'll take her," he told the guards simply.

Bláithín walked to my motel with me to grab my bag, so that we could go back to Wheelwright. She didn't say much; she only spoke when it couldn't be avoided.

I caught sight of Niall and Aodhan walking toward us as we left, belongings in hand. Niall held Liam easily in his arms. They all had a silver glow to them, their glamours hiding them from the eyes of passersby. I looked over at Bláithín, and when I squinted I saw she had a glamour on as well.

"Should I put on a glamour, too?" I asked her quietly, scrunching my face at the strangeness of the question.

She laughed. "Allison, you *are* glamoured."

"Oh," I looked at my skin, and for the first time realized that I had the same glow as the others. How could that have happened without me even knowing it?

I sighed, trying to focus on our next move. I assumed we'd be running—that made the most sense, I guessed— but I wasn't sure how I felt about being carried by Aodhan. He was so intimidating, and it had been awkward enough with my own father.

Liam looked so helpless lying in Niall's arms, and I realized that somehow in the past few days I'd actually grown to trust him. Maybe even care about him.

Aodhan narrowed his eyes at me, and I tried to even out my features. I didn't have a choice of who I went with, so I needed to just accept it.

"Liam made me go to sleep last time we...traveled. Do you know how to do that?" I asked.

Aodhan almost smiled. "I do. It would make it less harrowing for you, but I don't have to do it."

I gritted my teeth and held up my hands. "It's fine," I said.

With one last look at me, Niall disappeared into a run,

Bláithín on his heels.

Aodhan took a step toward me, and the last thing I knew he was staring hard into my eyes.

Chapter Nine

I'm standing at the top of the Magliaro's driveway, watching Ethan walk out his front door. He starts toward his truck but turns around, as if someone called his name.

I see myself walk out the door and over to where he's waiting. He wraps his arm around me and gives me a gentle squeeze. But when his fingers make contact with my skin, my form wavers. It's not me at all. It's a tall, ivory-skinned girl with long, brown hair and sapphire eyes.

Ethan hooks his finger in hers, and her features turn back into mine as they walk together toward his truck. When he turns his back to her, the corners of her mouth turn up into a grin, wicked and predatory.

I jerked awake to find myself propped up on an old wingback chair. Aodhan knelt on the wooden floor in front of me, his thick arms held out like he was about to shake me. I wasn't sure if his expression was fear or astonishment. He raised his eyebrows at me but didn't say a word as he rose to his feet.

The sitting room at Niamh's house was straight out of a museum of 18th-century living. There was a huge fireplace in front of me with a mural painted directly onto the wooden paneling above the mantel. The shelves held all manner of crockery, and on the various tables sat brass oil lamps.

I stood up slowly, wringing my hands as I walked to the window that looked out onto the barn. I could feel Aodhan watching me from the sofa across the room. I ran through the dream of Ethan in my mind, trying to make sense of it.

"What is it?" he asked, his voice gruff but not unkind.

"I had one of the dreams I told you about," I said.

I looked down at my clasped hands before continuing, "It was of a fr-friend of mine, Ethan. I saw him walking with...with me. Only, it *wasn't* me. The girl he was with was glamoured to look like me."

"Does that mean anything to you?" Aodhan asked.

"Well, I don't know. These dreams never really make much sense," I said.

"The Danaans don't think like humans. You must second-guess *everything*. Their actions often don't make sense, but they always do things for a reason. And if one of them has your friend, my guess would be they are trying to get your attention."

I pulled my phone out of my pocket. I had to call and check on Ethan. To my surprise, I actually had service. But his number went straight to voice mail. That wasn't a good sign.

I decided to try his parents' house. His father picked up, and I asked if Ethan was home.

"No, I haven't heard from him." He paused. "But didn't he leave with you not too long ago?"

My breath caught in my throat. He hadn't left with me, but if my dream was turning out to be true, he thought he had. I had to think fast.

"Uh, yeah. He just dropped me off, and now his phone is going to voice mail," I lied. "I can text him. Thanks, Mr. Magliaro."

I hung up and looked over at Aodhan. "They think Ethan's with me. I think Breanh really has taken him."

"Eithne and Diarmuid went back through the portal a few hours before we arrived. Your father needs a healer immediately, so I've arranged to go with him to Tír na n'Óg to find Eithne. We'll find your friend and bring him home, too."

He stood and gestured for me to follow him. I exhaled, and swallowed back my fears. I had to be stronger than that. "And what am I supposed to do? Just sit here and wait?"

Aodhan didn't answer. Instead, he led me outside, where Tagdh was opening the weathered wooden door of a flat-stoned entryway. The structure was dug into a low hillside, assembled with moss-covered stones held firmly in place by the earth surrounding them. A still unconscious Liam lay in the grass just to the left of the hill. Niall was talking in a low voice to Bláithín just a few feet away.

Tagdh turned around as we approached. He nodded respectfully at Aodhan.

Niall bent to gather Liam in his arms again, and he and Bláithín joined us at the door.

"We ready?" she asked.

"Let's go." Aodhan said. He nodded at me. *Okay, I guess that's my answer.*

Bláithín went in first, glancing back at us as she walked. Niall ducked through next, walking sideways to keep Liam's limbs from hitting the frame.

Inside the door, crumbling stone steps led down to a dim root cellar. The arched ceiling was made entirely of rock, and old wooden shelves lined the stone walls. Each one held dusty glass jars and bottles, some broken and lying on their sides.

An acute sense of dèja vu struck me as I looked around. This room was from one of my dreams, too. The only difference was that in my dream, Liam had been leading the way.

I turned and looked at Aodhan. He also was from my dream—the gigantic man, I was positive. He looked back at me blankly.

The room was only about fifteen feet long. At the far end, Bláithín placed her hand on the stones and blinding light filled the space. I reflexively turned away, but Niall and Bláithín walked into to the light and disappeared.

Squinting and averting my eyes to the floor, I took a deep breath and followed.

The light swallowed itself, and we appeared in a gathering room of sorts. In the center of the room was a wooden table long enough to seat ten. The edges were carved with spiraling flowers that matched the scrollwork on the chairs. The whitewashed ceiling arched up, supported by thick, knobby roots. The room itself felt wild, like a part of nature.

As I examined it, I realized that the tree that was

attached had actually grown to form the room's frame. Windows showed hints of trailing flowers in a multitude of colors just outside, and on the wall was a little alcove that held a sphere similar to the one I'd seen in my dream. I walked toward it, looking at the little shimmering ball. Inside were only bubbles that sparkled in the light.

Niall and Bláithín disappeared through a hallway in search of Eithne. No one had said it in quite as many words, but it was clearly urgent to remove the iron from his body. And judging by the pallor of his skin, the sooner the better.

Aodhan ran his finger along the flowers and looked up at me. "We need to be armed."

I laughed, not because the need for weapons was funny, but the idea of me *using* a weapon was ridiculous.

"I don't really know how to use any weapons."

My face flared at the look he gave me, as though what I said was the most preposterous thing he'd ever heard. He smoothed his hands over his buzz-cut and gestured for me to follow him.

He led me down the same hallway the others had gone through. As I walked, I felt disoriented, as if I went through too quickly and hadn't taken enough steps. I shook my head and looked back. The length of the hallway didn't match the amount of time it took to get through.

We entered a room similar in size and shape to the gathering room, but instead of a table, the room had couches and cushions arranged in a circle. Against the back wall, a stone staircase curved up to a second floor. As I followed Aodhan up, I lost my equilibrium and had to hold tight to the wooden railing to stay upright. He looked back at me, his eyebrows drawn together.

I laughed at myself, but it came out more like a shaky breath. "Give me a minute, I just got a little dizzy."

"Time and space are different in this realm," he explained. "Your body needs a chance to adjust."

At the top of the staircase we entered a room with bronze helmets decoratively set on stone pedestals. Aodhan walked over to kneel in front of a polished stone case. He opened it to reveal three bronze swords and two bronze daggers lying on a cushion.

"This was once Deaghlan's weapon collection. When he and Saoirse bonded he inherited the weapons of the High Court, but there hasn't been a need for them in a very long time."

"Which one is Deaghlan again?" I asked. My mind swirled with all the new names to remember.

Aodhan turned and looked at me, swallowing roughly. "Niamh and Aoife's father."

Bláithín appeared at the doorway then. "We need to go to the Bruidhean. Eithne isn't here."

Aodhan rose and handed me a scabbard before sliding one of the swords into a strap across his back.

He cast a look at Bláithín.

"In English, Bruidhean means Fairy Palace," she said. "It's the home of the King and Queen."

I nodded as I flipped the dagger in my hand. I wasn't sure what I'd be able to do with it.

"You never know what they'll do," Aodhan said, his voice thick with disdain. "It's best to be prepared."

I followed them out of the room, muttering to myself. "I guess I could poke someone just as well as anyone else."

The sky in Tír na n'Óg was bluer than I'd ever seen it at home. It was like stepping into Oz and I was Dorothy. Everything here was richer, more vibrant than I could have imagined.

Niamh's house was built into a low hill. The windows and doors were round and merry like an oversized hobbit hole. The lush flowers I'd seen through the window covered everything, making it nearly impossible to see what the actual house was built from.

I found it hard to focus on the fact that Liam's life was in jeopardy or that my mother and Ethan had been kidnapped by a psychotic faerie. Everything in Tír na n'Óg was mesmerizing.

The sound of the Danaan's boots hitting the dirt directed my gaze to the dusty path they walked. I took a deep breath and quickened my steps to catch up. Rich, moist air filled my lungs leaving a sweet taste like honey on my tongue.

Movement on the side of the path caught my attention. The grass and bushes swayed, but with more of a natural grace than by a breeze or wind. I brushed my fingertips along a flowering vine that hung between two low tree branches. I gasped—I could actually *feel* life pulsing from not only the vine, but the tree it hung from.

It was enough to alert the others several yards ahead. Aodhan's hand went immediately to the hilt of the sword at his back. He hurried over to me, and gave me a knowing look when he saw my fingers splayed across the vine.

"It's a bit of a shock, no? This realm is utterly different from ours. The plants, the wild creatures, they're all...*aware.*" He glanced again at where my hand had been. "They won't harm you. They're simply curious, I think." He reached out his hand to stroke the delicate leaves on the vine, then titled his head toward the others. "Come on. Time to go."

As we continued over the top of a grassy hill, I could see a valley with a sparkling river snaking through it. Beyond the river, the land was rippled with green hills, and speckled in each hill were doors and windows, similar to Niamh's. Farther along was a steeper hill, or maybe a low, green mountain.

"It's always just as breathtaking," Aodhan said, quiet enough that I could just make out his words.

"Is that the br—I can't remember what you called it." I could feel the flush rising to my face. "Is this where the king and queen live?" I rephrased.

"Yes, that would be the Bruidhean," Aodhan said over his shoulder. He continued walking after the others down the hillside, leading me toward god knows what.

Chapter Ten

Bláithín reached the round, wooden doors of what they called the Bruidhean first. She pulled on the bronze handle and ushered us in. Inside the doorway was an impressive entry hall. Niamh's advisor, Diarmuid, was walking up a stone staircase that curled around the room.

At the sound of the door, he looked over his shoulder at us. He smiled, apparently not surprised to see us, until he saw Niall carrying Liam in his arms. Then he turned and hurried down to us.

"He's been stabbed with a steel dagger," Bláithín explained. "When the dagger was removed, a piece broke off and is still deep in the wound."

"Follow me. Eithne is upstairs." Diarmuid led Niall up the stairs in a flash.

Bláithín turned and put her hand up. "We should wait here. I'm sure the queen will be here soon."

"You are quite right," called a lilting voice from the hallway under the staircase.

The skin tightened around Aodhan's eyes, and I looked

over Bláithín's shoulder, freezing at what I saw.

The woman from my dream.

The memory was nothing compared to reality. Dressed in a white gown embroidered with delicate green vines along the trim and waist, the queen of Tír na n'Óg was radiant. Her blonde hair was luminescent. Her skin milky white and flawless. But the most captivating thing about her was her eyes. The light made rainbows along their surfaces, like an opal.

As she came closer I started to raise my hand to touch her face, just barely stopping myself when I realized what I was doing.

"Welcome, Allison." Saoirse's smile drew me toward her like a flower drawn to the sun.

I couldn't speak.

After a moment of being trapped in her stare, Saoirse looked over my shoulder.

"It's been a while, Aodhan."

"Yes, my lady," Aodhan said.

Saoirse focused her smile back on me then, causing warmth and joy to radiate through my veins again.

"You're here to see Niamh?" she asked slowly, each syllable gliding from her lips.

After a beat, Aodhan spoke, the tension thick in his voice. "We realize Niamh already came to seek your counsel in finding Allison's mother, but Liam has been injured and needs care."

"Yes, Niamh has explained the situation to me," Saoirse replied, tilting her head slightly to one side. "Aoife has caused many problems."

I blinked at Saoirse, who smiled demurely back at me.

"Why don't we continue our talk in comfort?" Saoirse asked, walking out of the entryway without waiting for a response, her flowing gown and bell sleeves trailing behind her.

She led us into a gathering room with high ceilings, and like Niamh's house, the palace was framed by thick roots from a tree above the hill. Blue fabric was draped along the walls, and although there were no windows, tiny spheres of light were suspended to illuminate intricately embroidered flowers and trees. The effect was like a summer day, even though we were deep in the hillside.

Saoirse folded herself onto one of the plush divans, gesturing for us to each do the same. She met my gaze and smiled, and I was lost in the strange beauty of her eyes once again.

"Tell me about your dreams, Allison."

I licked my lips, trying to remember what dreams I was supposed to recall. "Well, sometimes I dream of things that might have happened in the past. But some of my dreams are of things that haven't happened, at least not yet."

Saoirse nodded, her sweet expression not changing. "You have the blood of my people. It isn't potent, but you are gifted with the Sight."

"I dreamed that my friend Ethan," I started to say, but the sound of footsteps and low laughter stopped me.

Two figures entered the room. Niamh froze in the entryway, her eyes wide. My breath was stolen by the laughing figure behind her.

My mother.

My mother was *laughing*. But when she stopped, her sparkling green eyes followed Niamh's gaze to where we sat. The moment our eyes met, time froze, and everything else fell away. This woman was—and yet was not—my mother.

"In Tír na n'Óg your mother is as she should be," Saoirse murmured.

I stood and walked to my mother, even though my whole body felt numb and tingly. She drew her lips in, just like she did when she was playing the violin. She really was my mother.

"Allison," she whispered as tears pooled in her eyes.

I felt my own tears welling as dozens of emotions buzzed around in my heart. Love, relief, awe.

Her arms came around me and I hugged her back, my own arms shaking. "I never thought…" She sniffled and laughed into my hair. "I never thought this could happen."

"I don't understand," I said, pulling back to look at Niamh.

Her eyes flicked between mine and Aodhan's. He sat completely still, staring straight ahead. The only thing that showed he wasn't a statue was the trembling muscle in his jaw.

"I promised your father that your mother would be safe," Niamh said. "But Breanh can read minds, like me. If I had told either of you that I was taking Elizabeth here, Breanh could have read it in your thoughts. He would have come after you, Allison."

For the first time since I'd entered the Bruidhean, I felt the haze lift from my brain. It was quickly replaced by anger.

"But, you let us worry," I said, inhaling deeply. "You locked us out and left us with Thunder Bay as our only hope...where Liam almost died!"

My mother gasped quietly. "Liam? He's here?"

"He's going to be okay, Mom," I said, rubbing her back. "He was already healing when we brought him here." I had no idea how true that was, but I'd spent my entire life being cautious of my mother's fragile mental state, and it was a habit.

I took a breath and refocused on Niamh and Saoirse, Aodhan's words sounding in my head. *They don't think like you. They're not human.*

I let it drop. "So, since both of my parents are here, can we break the geis?"

Saoirse sat calmly watching me from her perch, rubbing her finger lightly across her bottom lip. "From what I've seen, Aoife used a fháillan amulet infused with drops of Liam's and Elizabeth's blood for the geis. In order to break it, we need the amulet that binds it."

Frustration mingled with despair in my heart. The chance to bring my mother back was so close. "Do you know where the amulet is?" I asked.

Saoirse looked into my eyes. "The amulet is hidden in Aoife's home, but her lands have become polluted with iron and chemicals—it makes it difficult for even me to see."

I shook my head. No. There had to be a way. "But what if I—"

"Allison," Aodhan interrupted. "What about your friend?"

Ethan. Anger licked at my mind for becoming muddled again.

"Saoirse," I said. "That's another reason we're here. I dreamed of my friend Ethan the other night, and the girl he was with was glamoured to look like me. Something wasn't right about her—she looked at him... like a predator. And I think—"

"Perhaps we could take a walk, Allison?" Saoirse asked. "I have something I'd like to show you."

Aodhan cut in before I'd even opened my mouth to reply. "Wherever she goes, I go."

I didn't want to leave my mother, not when I'd just gotten her back. But I knew in my heart that Ethan was in danger—he had actually gone off with that girl, after all—and I needed to figure out a way to get to him.

"I'll still be here when you come back, Allison." My mother smiled at me, the way I'd been dreaming of since I was just a little girl. "And, I'd like to see your father."

Aodhan and I followed Saoirse through a door in the back of the hill. A stone path wound down to a lush garden nestled between the rises in the land. Trees heavily laden with fruit surrounded the garden walls, and the air smelled sweet like honeysuckle and apple blossoms, nearly making my mouth water.

Saoirse led us to the farthest end of the garden, where a

sparkling stream flowed into a pool at the bottom of one of the hills. The water in the rocky pool was as clear as pure glass. Saoirse gestured for me to sit on a smooth, stone bench along the shore.

Saoirse sat down by my side, folding her slender fingers on her lap. "This is Danu's Basin. It has been said that The Great Mother herself gained knowledge from this very pool before she traveled to The Land of Promise, *Magh Mell.*"

Aodhan stood in the shade of a giant tree, but I could see that his eyes were in constant motion as Saoirse and I spoke.

"You're worried about your friend?" she asked.

"Yes, Ethan."

"I am a Seer, but the future can change drastically with one simple decision. The visions I see in in the water, though, are absolute."

She held up her hands, and the water in the pool began to move in a circle like a whirlpool. Mist rose from its surface, and I looked over to Saoirse who had closed her eyes. She dropped her hands down, and as they fell, the mist cleared away. On the smooth surface of the water I could now see Ethan, walking into a room of six beautiful women. He was wearing only his jeans, and his eyes were dull, his smile bemused.

The woman I recognized from my dream led him to a low bed where the others all sat, laughing and smiling at him. They crawled on all fours to get closer to him, their cold, bright eyes filled with lust and something else I couldn't decipher. They reached out with greedy fingers to touch him and stroke his skin. So many voices were speaking, too fast to understand what they were saying.

I closed my eyes, trembling with hurt and shock.

"She's seen *enough*," Aodhan said from his place under the tree.

Saoirse raised her hands, and the mist reappeared. When she folded them back in her lap, we were once again looking at the clear pool.

I shook my head. "What *was* that?"

"That was Aoife's home. It appears that Breanh has provided himself with a new bargaining chip. Since your mother disappeared, he must be holding Ethan in exchange for Aoife."

"But, I can't give him Aoife. I don't even know where she is."

"No, it is for the best if she remains in the fey globe for now," Saoirse agreed.

"Who were they? And why were they doing that to him?" I asked. Despite the erotic way they touched him, there was something twisted and wrong in their eyes. Hot anger—and a bit of jealousy—shot through me. *If they hurt him…*

Saoirse closed her eyes and sat still and silent. When she reopened them, she looked into my eyes. "You must go to Breanh. You are the one who must save Ethan."

I looked up at Aodhan who remained impassive. My heart was forming ice crystals as I tried to understand what all of this meant. "Has what I saw already happened?"

Saoirse shook her head. "No, there is still time. But if this plays out, Ethan will become enthralled to whoever he is intimate with."

I ground my teeth together, trying to keep the anger at

bay.

"Don't tell me you're having a party without me?" an unfamiliar voice said from the path.

I looked over my shoulder to see a man walking toward us. He smiled as he approached Saoirse. Like all of the Danaans, he was stunning. His hair was glossy black, his jawline pale and chiseled. When he smiled, it was smooth and rich, like butter on freshly baked bread.

"Deaghlan, this is Allison," Saoirse said, her lips forming an enigmatic smile.

When I met his curious blue lapis eyes, longing coursed through my veins. Somewhere deep in my mind I knew that looking into someone's eyes shouldn't cause me to come undone like this, but my body wasn't listening to the tiny voice in my mind. When he reached for my hand, I only stared at it for a minute before realizing I was supposed to give it to him. When he grinned at me, it was like he had a secret and he liked it that way.

"Surely she isn't *just* a human," Deaghlan said.

Saoirse smiled. "You sense the mark of our people on her, too?"

Deaghlan waved his hands dismissively, but didn't take his eyes off me. Something in the way he had scoffed at my being "just a human" caused the fog in my head to clear.

"As much as I enjoy being the topic of this discussion, I need to go to find Ethan."

Then I noticed the way Aodhan stood, so rigid with tension he might snap. "Right. We appreciate your help, Saoirse, and we'll return this way when our business is through."

"Aodhan! I didn't see you there," Deaghlan exclaimed. "Don't leave on my account. I meant no offense to the girl."

Aodhan's calm facade stayed firmly in place. "Of course not. But Allison and I really must be going."

Aodhan walked down the little hill and grabbed my elbow, a bit forcefully.

"Surely you aren't leaving before the night rains? I insist you join us for food and drink and wait to leave until the first light of day," Deaghlan said. He smirked as he looked at Aodhan, but his tone was commanding.

I opened my mouth to argue, but the look on Aodhan's face made me shut it immediately. His expression said no one argued with the king of Tír na n'Óg.

Chapter Eleven

I couldn't decide what the texture was like, exactly. It felt smooth, like silk, but it was soft and comfortable like cotton. The way it hugged my skin was something like spandex, but it was flattering in a way that spandex could never be. The dress fit me so perfectly, like it had been made just for me. The color was a glacier blue, precisely the same shade as my eyes.

I shook my head, trying to get my thoughts to refocus. For the moment, my parents were safe. My mother had not returned from her reunion with Liam. I desperately wanted to know how he was, but no one would tell me anything.

"He's like a wolf," Aodhan muttered from where he sat at my side. His gaze flickered around the gathering room, constantly vigilant.

"Hmm?" I asked, wondering if he was even speaking to me.

"At one point, I worshiped Deaghlan. He seemed so *strong* when I first met him."

I followed his gaze to where Deaghlan stood among a

group of other Danaans.

"Don't let him fool you. Don't think for a *second* that he doesn't see every move you make."

"You really do hate them, don't you?" I asked, knowing I was crossing some unspoken line but not letting it stop me.

"I won't let myself care about them enough to hate them," he said, leaning back. He crossed his arms and went back to scanning the room.

Beautiful men and women were scattered around, laughing and dancing, eating and drinking. The women wore dresses similar to mine, floating in flowing jewel-toned gowns of sapphire, amethyst, and emerald. The men wore embroidered tunics in earth tones of moss, bark, and sand with pants tucked into their boots.

Lights twinkled from the spheres high in the ceiling, sparkling off silver chalices and platters as the sounds of laughter and music mingled in my mind with the scent of ripe fruit and fresh cream. Plates were piled with scones topped with berries ripe enough to burst, and the silver cups were full of a shimmering golden liquid. My senses were overwhelmed—I felt dizzy trying to take in the extravagance of this world.

When a plate and cup were placed on the table in front of me, Aodhan leaned in to speak in my ear. "Eat only what you must, and drink very little. You don't want to get a taste for their food; you'll never want to eat human food again."

I stared longingly at my plate, and a voice spoke from behind me.

"I hope you don't think I'm rude, Allison," Deaghlan

said smoothly, taking the chair on my other side.

He chuckled at my startled expression. I wanted so badly to be annoyed by his smugness, but his eyes were so deep and so blue that I couldn't look away.

"You're my guest, and I haven't paid you any attention," he went on.

I pulled my eyes away and focused on the bowls of flowers in the center of the table. "No," I answered, trying to put an edge in my voice. "I don't even want to be here, so it doesn't matter."

Deaghlan laughed again, and I knew it was because rather than sounding firm, my words came out shaky.

"You'll need to eat and get some sleep so that you'll be of use to your friend, Allison."

The way he said my name caused a shiver to pass through me. I stared down at Aodhan's fisted hands as they rested on the table. The muscles in his forearms were taut, showing how he reacted to Deaghlan's presence.

Aodhan's face was impassive as ever, but for a moment, I noticed how he watched Niamh across the table. The fire in his eyes skirted between hatred and longing, but as if he sensed me watching him, he went back to scanning the room.

I needed to get myself away from Deaghlan if I were to be able to think straight. He was too beautiful, painfully so. When I looked at him, every thought I had about my parents and Ethan scattered and all I could do was drown in his eyes. This attraction to Deaghlan and Saoirse, all of the Danaans, was unnatural. But I only realized what was happening when they weren't speaking to me.

And I had more important things to worry about. I

needed to come up with a way to see Liam and my mother, and save Ethan. And Aodhan was right—not just Deaghlan, but all of the Danaans were watching every single move I made.

"I need a moment," I told no one in particular. "I need a *woman's* moment," I said hoping this was enough to keep them from asking any questions.

Deaghlan smoothed the sleeves of his tunic, only the slightest touch uncomfortable with my words. "Eithne," he called out, and the girl I'd met in Wheelwright appeared immediately at his side.

He looked up at her charmingly. "Allison needs assistance. You'll take care of her, won't you?"

Eithne bowed her head at him, and I rose quickly to follow her out of the gathering room. She didn't meet my eyes as she led me away, which made me uncomfortable. I wasn't sure what it was, but I felt like she was afraid of me.

"Eithne," I said quietly, stopping as I walked through the entryway with the stone staircase. She stopped in front of me, her sandy-colored hair forming a curtain around her face.

"Is my...is Liam going to be okay?" I asked.

She turned partially around, peeking up at me from behind her feathery lashes. "Liam is going to be fine. He had a shard of iron in his wound, which has been removed. He will sleep for another day before his body is healed. And Niall took the iron out of Tír na n'Óg before it did any more damage."

I nodded, and she led me up the stone steps and down a hallway lit with the mysterious little balls of light—fey lights, I'd learned they were called. A few doors were closed along each wall, and at the end, another set of steps curved up to another floor. As I climbed the steps, a shifting feeling stopped me. I leaned against the cool stones and squeezed my eyes shut.

Eithne was watching me warily when I opened them. I laughed quietly, trying to regain my equilibrium. Breathing through my nose, I continued to the top. I followed her into a room to the right of the landing where stone basins lined the wall on one side and three curtains covered what looked like alcoves carved into the stone of the other.

"Wait, I don't really need to use the ladies room. I'm sorry," I said. I should've said something sooner. "I really wanted to see Liam. Please take me to see him?" I asked, hoping she could see how important it was by my expression.

"Very well," she said, and I almost asked her to repeat herself. It seemed too easy.

"Eithne?"

She continued averting her eyes. "Yes?"

"Have I done something to make you uncomfortable?"

She met my eyes. I could see that she was afraid of something, but I couldn't tell what.

"If Aoife finds out that I've helped you..." she trailed off.

"Aoife? What does Aoife have to do with me?"

Eithne's eyebrows shot up, and a little sound escaped her lips. "I'm not sure what you know about how Liam and I met..."

"I don't know anything about it," I said even though Liam had mentioned something about it. My interest was piqued by what Eithne would tell me.

"Well"—she looked around nervously—"I was once Aoife's handmaiden. When she would leave Tír na n'Óg it was my duty to take care of Liam. I am her cousin, and I was the only one she felt she could trust, you see.

"I helped him when I could. He would go back into the human realm, and I would sneak him back without Aoife's notice. But one day, she felt I'd betrayed her. I knew too many of her secrets, she said, and she banished me to the human realm."

I gaped at her. Niamh had told me that Aoife was known for her temper, but I wasn't sure how Aoife could hurt her now.

"Liam and Niamh have imprisoned Aoife, though," I said.

She nodded. "Yes, but there are eyes everywhere. Deaghlan won't allow her to stay in the sphere for much longer, and when she finds out you're here, and that I've helped you..."

"Is it because I'm Liam's daughter that you think she'll be angry?"

Eithne's eyes widened in fear. "I can't say anymore, Allison. Please."

"Wait," I said, holding my hands up, trying to placate her. There was something I was missing. I needed to figure out what Eithne was so afraid of.

"Why will Aoife be so angry?" I asked again, begging her to confide in me.

"Because she made me keep your existence a secret. I don't know how Liam and Niamh tracked you, but when Aoife finds out, I know I'll pay for it."

"But you weren't the one who told them about me.

Everyone knows that."

"Oh, it doesn't matter. When I hid you for her, I was so careful. I never understood how she could give away such a beautiful creature, but she detested you. Liam didn't even know about you, but she was seething with jealousy over a harmless baby girl—"

"I'm not following," I interrupted. "What do you mean you hid me? I didn't think Aoife even knew about me. Niamh and Liam didn't know about me when they showed up looking for my mother."

"Your mother?" Eithne said, tilting her head to one side.

I got the distinct feeling we were talking about two completely different scenarios, but I had no idea how to untangle the threads of the story she'd just told me.

"Yes. Liam came to my grandparents' house looking for my mother, Elizabeth—"

If Eithne's expression could have become more horrified, it did then. "Elizabeth is your mother?" she asked slowly, some of her confusion disappearing.

"Uh, yes." I said, shaking my head. "You've lost me again."

"Oh, Allison," she muttered, covering her face in her hands. "Please, forget what I've told you. It is best for everyone if you pretend we hadn't spoken."

Eithne clearly thought I was someone else. From the sound of things, she thought Aoife was my mother. I shook my head. I needed to calm her down.

I put my hand on her shoulder until she uncovered her face and looked at me. "I don't know who you think I am, Eithne, but right now I have to see my father. Can you take me to him? Please?"

Her face relaxed a fraction and she nodded. "Follow me."

Liam lay in a bed motionless, covered with soft blankets pulled up to his chest. His eyes were closed, but he'd regained his normal coloring. He looked like he was just sleeping soundly.

My mother sat in a chair that had been pulled up right next to the bed. She gazed down at him, her face a collage of different emotions. The strongest by far was love.

I sat on the arm of the chair and placed my hand slowly on her shoulder. When she looked up at me, she smiled again, her eyes reflecting the light like sea glass in the sun.

"I never dreamed we would all be in the same room, Allison. It was too much to hope for." She lifted her hand to Liam's face but wasn't able to break through the geis to touch him.

"Were you aware of everything that went on around you? All of this time?" I asked, not sure if she would know what I meant.

"Yes," she whispered, pain evident on her face. "It has been like being stuck in a room while I watched your life unfold on a television. All of this time I've been trapped in my own mind, screaming, but nobody could hear me."

"Oh, Mom…once Ethan is safe, I'm going to figure out how to make this right."

"Allison, you should return before they notice you are missing," Aodhan said, appearing in the doorway.

I smiled at my mother and kissed her cheek. "I'll be back soon."

Aodhan brought me back to the gathering room where most of the Danaans were now dancing in the center of the room. Deaghlan sat at the head of the table with Saoirse, both leaning back in their chairs watching the dancers.

They were dancing closer than before, more intimately. Their bodies pressed tightly together, moving with each other. As the music played on, they changed partners and entwined their bodies with no shame or self-consciousness. Liam told me that, by nature, the Danaans weren't a monogamous race. Some had a bondmate, like Diarmuid and Eithne, but they considered intimacy something that wasn't restricted to any one individual.

Aodhan and I went back to our seats, and I wondered how much more time I had to spend here before it was considered polite to go to the bedroom that awaited me. The morning couldn't come soon enough. The panic was setting in, and I was forced to have faith in Saoirse's visions that I would get to Ethan before any permanent damage was done.

"Perhaps a dance would take your mind off of your friend?" Deaghlan appeared at my side, startling me.

I shook my head, refusing to look up into those eyes. "I think it's time for me to get some sleep," I said, watching the way Niamh stared at Aodhan over the shoulder of her dance partner.

For a moment, Deaghlan didn't respond. "Would you like an escort?" he asked, his words smooth and tantalizing like honey, but with a touch of something sharper.

Aodhan snorted softly. "It's no trouble for me to take her to her room. I'll be going too."

"Very well," Deaghlan responded.

I was more than a little afraid of the unhappiness of his tone.

Gram sits on the couch, her hair pulled back in a bun that's coming undone. Her eyes are downcast, and she's holding a picture of my mother in her hands, worrying the edges with her fingers.

I can see Pop is sitting in the kitchen, staring off into space as Aunt Jessie tries to talk to him. His eyes look sunken in, his skin so pale. His eyebrows knit together, and he closes his eyes tight. His hand flies to his chest and Aunt Jessie shouts at him, asking him what's wrong. His eyes slacken, and his mouth opens as he starts to slip out of the chair.

I woke with a start. The bed was so comfortable, but I knew I wasn't at home. Memories began flooding back to me. I was in Tír na n'Óg. Liam had been stabbed. My mother was herself, if only temporarily. And Ethan was captured by sadistic faeries who wanted to do all kinds of bad things to him.

Then, the memory of the dream hit me: my grandfather was having a heart attack.

I jumped up out of the bed, just as Niamh walked into the room. Her expression wasn't the typical haughty one I was used to. She looked like she had something to tell me.

"I saw your dream," she began.

"Oh?" I asked as grabbed my clothes off the table next to my bed.

"Not all of your visions will come true, you know."

I froze after popping my shirt over my head. "That hasn't happened?" I asked.

Niamh shook her head. A huge weight lifted off of my shoulders. That meant I might still have time.

"Now I just need to get Ethan away from the seductress fairies at Aoife's brothel or whatever it is, we can figure out what is needed to break the geis, and we can all go home," I said, yanking a sock onto my foot. Frustration was setting in—I was surprised I hadn't snapped sooner.

"Don't worry about your grandfather, Allison. My mother has sent decoys to take your place while you're here."

"What do you mean by decoys?" I asked, scrunching my face around the word.

"Two of my handmaidens and one of my guards are glamoured to pass as you, Ethan, and your mother."

I stared at her for a second, unsure how to respond.

She huffed a little and waved dismissively. "We have to keep up appearances. I know it feels like you've only been in Tír na n'Óg for a single day, but in your world it's been about three weeks."

I shook my head and stood. "Aodhan mentioned the time difference. That is so bizarre."

"Maybe, but it's true."

As she was speaking, I caught a glimpse of Aodhan standing just outside the doorway. Before last night I might not have picked up on the pinprick of emotion in his eyes as he watched Niamh. As it was, I wasn't sure I was reading the whole situation correctly, but something was there.

"We should be going," Aodhan said firmly. Any emotion I thought I'd seen burned away as fast as it had appeared. Niamh gave me a tiny nod and quietly slipped past him.

"We've been given provisions to last two days," he said without another look at Niamh.

His face screwed up as he muttered under his breath, "However long that really is."

I'd never really been able to achieve comfortable silence with anyone other than my family before. For whatever reason, people feel this innate need to fill the silence with meaningless chatter, but Aodhan led me down the hill quietly. I wasn't sure exactly why he hadn't offered to run, but I had a feeling it was because he needed some time to think too.

Seeing my mother the way I'd always heard her described—smiling and radiant—had been one of the best moments of my life. Leaving her so soon was hard, especially after learning that as soon as we set foot out of Tír na n'Óg she'd go back to the way I'd always known her.

The memories of Ethan with all of those women and what they could do to him burned my eyelids. I couldn't let him become like my mother. His family would be devastated, and I still had a chance to prevent it from happening. I didn't know how, but Saoirse's words made me hopeful that she had seen a future in which I'd saved Ethan.

I heard chattering then as I walked past a smattering of ash trees. On a low branch, a squirrel watched me with intelligent eyes. I thought of how Aodhan had said the vines were curious about me. Apparently, this critter was also.

Aodhan walked several paces ahead, tense and alert to every sound and movement. The way he moved reminded me of a panther. I wondered if he had always been this agile, or if it was the effect of being in Tír na n'Óg for so long.

"Aodhan," I called ahead.

He stopped and turned. "Aye?" he asked.

"I was just wondering what your *gift* is?" All the Danaans had some kind of ability, but he hadn't mentioned his yet.

He snorted, turning his head away. "My gift," he muttered as he started walking again.

"Sorry," I said, embarrassed for having brought it up.

"I suppose the gift you speak of would be my strength. I'm stronger than most of the others, faster probably, too."

He slowed his pace so that we were walking side by side.

I nodded, but he wasn't done.

"I can do a little of everything they can do, I think. I can use glamour to stay hidden—so that would be the mind control. And I can sometimes, but not often, move things with my thoughts. It's sort of like singing. Anyone can sing, some just do it better than others."

To hear him speak openly like that was surprising and wonderful. He had such a deep accent, too. I wondered what his life had been like growing up in Ireland so long ago. And what had made him decide to come with me.

"You want to know why I agreed to help you," he said as he rubbed one hand across the fuzz growing on his chin.

I laughed nervously. "Did you read my mind?"

Enough time passed that I didn't think he would continue, but he surprised me again.

"I had a family once," he began, looking over at me. "Three brothers, two sisters. My father was the chieftain of our clan. I spent most of my life dreaming of ways to make the English pay for what they were doing to my country.

"We fought for our freedom, but in the end we were forced to leave our home, made to flee like thieves in the night. Once my family had made it to safety, I took one last sweep of our camp. I vaguely remember being shot in the back," he closed his eyes, remembering. "I can still see the English scum spitting on me as I lay face-down in the mud. All I could do was lay there and wait to die.

"After the English left, I heard a voice whispering in my mind. I opened my eyes, and Niamh was there. In that moment I forgot about pain, forgot about my family. There was only *her*.

"By the time I met Liam, hundreds of years had passed. Everyone I'd ever known was dead and gone." He shook his head slowly. "It hadn't even occurred to me to care."

I didn't say anything in response—no words would be enough.

"There's a stream just ahead, we should stop for a drink." Aodhan started off the path, and I followed, my heart aching for all that he'd lost.

Everything in Tír na n'Óg felt like it was the way nature intended: bright blue sky during the day, soft misty rain at night. The grass was a lush green carpet rolling over the hills and smoothing out over the plains. Flowers and fruit grew everywhere you looked, all bursting with color and crisp fragrance.

But when we came to a wall of twisting brambles, it didn't feel anything like the beauty I'd seen so far. There was a sense of foreboding seeping out of the thorny vines.

"I don't remember this being here," Aodhan said as he paced the wall, looking for a way through. He attempted to loosen the snarled vines, but they wouldn't budge. He pulled a dagger out of his belt and began sawing at it.

"It's tedious," he said. "But these vines are immovable, and I can't see another way through."

I slid the dagger out of the scabbard that hung on my hip. The vines felt like dry bones rattling together as I cut them away. The thorns bit at my skin, and the smell coming out of the vines caused black dots to blur my vision, but I kept hacking away.

Aodhan cut a small path ahead, and I struggled to keep up with him. Thorns snagged my sleeves, and I wrestled the dagger through to free them. My hands were sliced and stinging, and when I looked up Aodhan was moving farther and farther away from me. I willed my feet to move faster and stumbled forward. I landed hard on the thorny ground. My vision swam, and I squeezed my eyes closed.

"Aodhan," I gasped, but there was no response.

Panic blossomed in my chest. I had to keep moving forward. I needed to find Aodhan. But my joints were locking up, making it difficult to do anything more than draw ragged breaths. I tried calling out to him again, but my voice came out as little more than a croak. I couldn't let it end like this, curled up in a web of brittle vines and thorns.

As I finished that thought, I heard a low moan come from ahead. I pushed my leaden legs up from beneath me, moving as best I could toward the sound.

When I found Aodhan, he was tangled in a mass of coiled vines. His arms and face were sliced open even worse than mine, and his bloody lips were parted. I knelt beside him, carefully cutting away the vines that ensnared him. It was like trying to cut down an oak tree with a butter knife.

I could feel him watching me as I worked, and after a few minutes, he became more coherent and wriggled his arms free.

"Get back," he whispered. I scrambled away as he tore

himself free of the net of branches and vines.

I leaned back on my elbows and inhaled the sickly sweet air. The edge of the thorny forest was only twenty feet away.

I started to tell Aodhan how close we were, but he didn't give me a chance. "Come on," he said, holding out his bloody hand to help me to my feet. "It's time."

Chapter Twelve

Beyond the briars and thorns, the ground was covered in dry, brown grass that crackled when we walked over it. Trees with no leaves dotted the landscape, their limbs reaching up to the sky in a silent plea for mercy. The ground turned rockier, and the trees were replaced by stout bushes that resembled steel wool.

The sun was hot and unforgiving in the jaundiced yellow sky, but we didn't even stop for a drink. The scent of salty sea air mixed with sulfur got stronger the farther we walked. We came to the edge of a steep cliff before Aodhan spoke again. His voice was barely audible over the crash of waves below.

"The entrance to Aoife's house is on the face of this cliff. The path is steep, so stay alert."

I looked over the ledge and down the narrow path, the wind whipping strands of hair in my eyes. I saw the gaping mouth of a cave halfway down to the rocky shore. Aoife had chosen the perfect place to live if she didn't want visitors.

I followed close on Aodhan's heels. As I walked, I leaned my body into the rocky wall.

When we reached the cave, I could only see about five feet inside before the path was swallowed up by darkness. Aodhan walked in, and after three steps, a chain of fey lights blinked on in a domino effect, lighting the cavern within.

I hurried after him. The cave entrance was charcoal gray and smooth, but as we walked deeper inside, we came to a corridor carved with intricate scrollwork, like trees with long curly-cue branches. The corridor came to an end with two crescent-shaped wooden doors. Aodhan opened one side with no trouble—we must be expected. I shivered at the thought.

Inside was a high-ceilinged entryway, lit by dozens of fey lights lining the walls. Beautiful spiral designs were carved into every surface. It didn't smell like the sea in here; there wasn't really a smell at all, just clean air. But it was quiet, and each step we took felt like the beat of an ominous drum.

Three doors led out of the entryway. I looked over at Aodhan for instruction, and he headed for the one directly in front of us.

A gasp escaped my lips as we entered the room. I remembered this place from my dream of Liam and Aoife. A man sat casually across the room—the same one I had dreamed of standing there with a black bird on his arm, smirking at me.

Breanh.

"Welcome, Allison. I'm so pleased you came," he said, a wicked grin spreading across his features. His black hair was shoulder length, framing his angular face.

At first I couldn't think of anything to say. I just stared at him until I sensed how much he enjoyed my discomfort. I looked up at Aodhan, but he just stared blankly at Breanh.

"Where's Ethan?" I asked, my voice as firm as I could make it.

"Oh, Ethan is fine. More than fine, you might say." The look of delight on his face increased as he spoke. Breanh took a step toward us, and I shrunk back, which only seemed to add to his pleasure.

"I must tell you…I'm impressed you made it through those nasty vines. They tend to be such a *problem*," he said with mock sincerity. "It's just too bad Aodhan wasn't so lucky."

Before I could say aloud that this guy was a total lunatic, Aodhan's form wavered beside me. I came close to screaming when I realized the man by my side was not Aodhan at all, but a complete stranger wearing a glamour.

Icy cold panic ran through me as Breanh looked on with another cruel smirk.

"What have you done with him?" I whispered.

He leaned forward on the balls of his feet, as though he was savoring my fear. "Aodhan took a terrible fall into a pit below the vines. I do hope he'll make it out soon. I'd love to see him."

"You're a monster." I took a deep breath, forcing myself to focus on the fact that Aodhan was still alive. I needed to find Ethan before he was completely enthralled by any of those women, then I would somehow find Aodhan in the thorny vines.

"This doesn't have to be painful, Allison," he said,

speaking each word slowly.

"I just want to bring Ethan home," I said, hating the way my voice sounded so small.

"Of course you do." His words dripped with false sympathy. "And you will have him just as soon as Aoife is returned here."

"You think *I* know where Aoife is? Last I knew, Liam and Niamh captured her in a fey globe and gave it to Deaghlan."

With a flick of Breanh's wrist a curtain at the opposite end of the room lifted. "I believe you can be persuaded to find out more."

Behind the curtain, my nightmare came to life. On a low bed covered with silky sheets lay Ethan. Tangled up in his limbs were the women from my dream. They all ran their hands along his naked body, making sounds of lust and longing. His eyes were closed, and his lips were parted as they kissed his arms and stroked his thighs.

The girl who had been glamoured as me ran her tongue from his navel to his clavicle and turned her head to smirk at me.

My knees went weak, and I held onto the wall to keep my balance. If he slept with one of them—I shuddered at the thought—he'd end up addicted to her, the way my mother was addicted to my father. He could end up schizophrenic, too, or worse. The room grew hotter as I struggled to breathe.

"As you can see, Ethan is a bit preoccupied. I'm sure while we wait, you and I can come to an arrangement of some sort."

"Ethan!" I shouted, my chest starting to heave in panic.

"Ethan, look at me!"

Breanh laughed, slowly clapping his hands. Ethan didn't open his eyes but rolled his head back as the women continued nipping and tasting his skin.

Unable to watch anymore, I ran toward the bed.

"Ethan, listen to me!"

Before I made it halfway, Breanh grabbed me. He chuckled in my ear as he gripped my neck. "You actually think Ethan would prefer you?" He laughed. "I can be very patient, Allison. And you have no idea how much I will enjoy getting you to cooperate."

The sound of footsteps behind us surprised Breanh. He turned around, taking me with him.

"Just what do you have in mind, Breanh?" The woman standing there had her eyebrow arched up over one of her bright azure eyes as she waited for a response. Her black hair was loose and cascaded over the shoulders of her deep navy gown. At the base of her throat was a silver amulet on a delicate silver chain.

Breanh's hold on me loosened, and I sucked in a deep breath.

"Aoife. You're here at last," he crooned to her.

"Answer the question," she said, not moving.

"I would do anything to get you back where you belong, of course."

"I see," she said coldly. "Then let her go."

Breanh's arms fell to his sides. Without pausing to consider what was happening, I ran to Ethan. He lay alone on the bed now—the females had apparently scattered when Aoife arrived. His head was on a pillow, and his eyes were closed. Fingers trembling, I pulled the sheet up to cover his body before turning back to Breanh and Aoife.

"Aoife," Breanh began, glancing over to where I sat.

"Don't," Aoife cut him off. "How could you bring her here?" She flung her hand toward me.

Breanh's eyes widened as he struggled to answer her.

"I-I told you I would have done anything..."

"The last thing I want is for Liam to know about her," she said.

"But..." The glare she shot him silenced him.

I secretly enjoyed watching as Breanh transformed from a ruthless brute to a whimpering coward as Aoife paced in a slow circle around him.

"Every time the responsibility to take charge falls on you, you create more problems than you started with. First with Liam and the human, then with the imbeciles in Canada." She shook her head and came to a stop directly behind him.

Breanh swallowed hard and waited for her to continue. Aoife moved in closer to him, standing flush against his back, and trailed one finger up his arm. His eyes fluttered as he inhaled a shaky breath.

"If Liam finds out he has a daughter, do you know what that means?"

"But, I didn't—"

She tapped his chest with her finger. "Answer the question."

Breanh inhaled as she trailed her hand from his pectoral muscles down to his abdomen.

"It means I lose everything," she whispered. "Again."

Breanh let out a grunt and swayed on his feet for a moment before collapsing into a heap on the floor. Sticking out of his back was the jeweled hilt of a dagger. I squeezed my eyes shut, once again grasping in my mind for a way out of my current predicament. I was within an arm's length of Ethan, although he was still in some eerie lust-filled oblivion, and Aodhan was trapped in a forest of vines and thorns.

Aoife sidestepped Breanh and walked over to the bed where I sat beside Ethan's still form. She tapped her lip thoughtfully and narrowed her eyes.

"You will be easy enough to get rid of. Provided we have no more problems."

I didn't think she was actually speaking to me, but rather thinking out loud. I stood, hoping that I looked braver than I felt. I clasped my hands behind my back to hide the trembling.

"How did you get out of the fey globe?" I asked, struggling to keep my composure.

Her eyebrow arched again. "It seems my mother doesn't subscribe to the whole *imprison Aoife* plan."

"Saoirse let you go?" That made no sense. Why would Saoirse let Aoife just go free? She'd admitted to the trouble her daughter caused and the harm it did.

"Tell me where Liam is"—with a frustrated huff, Aoife's eyes flickered to Ethan—"and I won't harm a hair on this boy's pretty little head."

"Liam is lying in a bed unconscious right now because one of *your* crazy guards stabbed him with an iron blade."

A flash of concern showed in her eyes before she rearranged her features into a coy smile.

"I must admit, Samantha…this is an exquisite human you've got here," Aoife said as she ran her eyes down

Ethan's exposed chest.

"Samantha?" I asked. "Who's Samantha?"

Her eyes darted to mine. "Isn't that what the humans named you?"

"My name is Allison."

"Hmm, no matter." Aoife blinked. "Come, we must get you back home to Thunder Bay before Liam wakes up. I'll deal with him then."

"What are you talking about?" I asked.

"I need you out of Tír na n'Óg before Liam wakes up. Breanh was a fool for bringing you here, but once you're back in Thunder Bay I can straighten everything out."

"Straighten what out?" I asked. "I don't understand."

"I have lost the upper hand with Liam. He can't find out about you, too. Humans are sentimental about their children. He'll wonder why I never told him about you." She waved her hand dismissively.

A faint buzz began in my ears at her words. I could hear Eithne sobbing that I must forget everything she had said, and then it all clicked. Aoife had given birth to Liam's child. Another child. And, like Eithne, Aoife thought I was her.

A pinpoint of hope ignited in my heart as I looked at Aoife's waiting expression. "I don't live in Thunder Bay. I'm not your daughter, either. My mother is Elizabeth. And she is with Liam right now, nursing him back to health."

Just as her lips parted in understanding, Aoife grabbed me by the throat. I struggled against her, but she had a firm grip as she pulled me to her face.

"I will enjoy killing you, then."

I tried to speak, but her fingers were crushing my

windpipe. Frantically, I fumbled along my belt for my dagger. Stars were dancing in front of my eyes as I pulled it out of the sheath and, with all my strength, stabbed it into her side.

Aoife cried out, and let go of my throat. I coughed and gasped, my lungs desperate for air. She tilted her head to one side and laughed cruelly.

"He'll never love you if you kill his child," I croaked. I knew it was a stretch, but I had to use her obsession with Liam against her; it was my only chance.

Indecision played across her features. "He'll never know it was me," she hedged.

From somewhere close I could hear the pounding of footsteps and a deep voice calling my name.

Aoife's eyes grew wide with panic as she scanned around the room. "Who else knows you're here?"

"Aodhan came here with me." I barely recognized the sound of my own voice.

Aoife grabbed a fistful of my t-shirt, pulling me toward her again. "You won't say a word of this to anyone," she whispered, her eyes boring into mine.

I licked my lips and nodded, feeling a little strange as I watched her pupils dilate. *A word, never a word to anyone.*

Then, with a glance over her shoulder, Aoife disappeared.

Seconds later, Aodhan charged into the room, looking around in alarm. When his eyes settled on me, I sunk down onto the bed. The adrenaline that had been coursing through my body had fled, leaving me drained.

Aodhan looked down at Breanh lying in a heap on the floor and back up at me. I let him draw whatever conclusions he would. It was easier at that point than trying to come up with a story of my own.

"Well," he said, a tiny smile playing at his lips as he walked over to where I sat with Ethan. "It looks like you didn't need me after all."

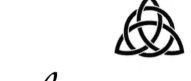

Chapter Thirteen

I sat in the chair like my mother had the night before to watch my father sleep. Ethan now lay in his place.

His eyes were closed, and his breaths even. There was a shadow on his cheeks. I'd never seen him with stubble before—if I didn't know better I'd think he was just sleeping.

But I did know better.

Aodhan had carried him all the way back to the Bruidhean. He'd used mind magic to get Ethan to sleep, but the glazed expression on his face was still vivid in my memory. I forced myself not to think about the Danaan woman tracing her finger down his jawline.

Aodhan stood guard at the door while we waited for Deaghlan to come alter Ethan's memories. It felt very wrong to let them tamper with his mind, but there wasn't much of a choice. If we let him go back to Stoneville as he was, he'd think the women were just a dream, but he'd also be missing a three week chunk of memories. A day and half in Tír na n'Óg meant we'd missed nearly a month back home.

A dark brown curl fell over Ethan's eye, and I reached out to smooth it back.

Saoirse and Niamh had been here a little while ago. Niamh had showed me, what had happened while we were away from reality so I could play along when we returned. Saoirse's watery basin was pretty handy when you needed to get caught up to speed on what you'd missed in your life.

The story was that I'd found my mother sitting by the Duck Pond halfway between our house and the house Joanne had grown up in. Life had gone back to normal after that, or as normal as life can be when it's a bunch of faeries disguised as you and the people you care about. Both Ethan and I had come down with "mono" to keep our interactions with others limited. I could just imagine all the jokes about us both coming down with the kissing disease.

Pop had spent a lot of time going to the doctor. He'd been feeling some discomfort in his chest, and I watched Gram tell fake-Allison that Pop would be fine, that the doctor visits were "just to be on the safe-side."

Aodhan cleared his throat, announcing Deaghlan's arrival and breaking me out of my thoughts.

As soon as he entered the room, Deaghlan's eyes found mine. He walked toward me, and I couldn't make myself look away. I could feel each step he took in my pulse as he got closer. Aodhan had said Deaghlan was like a wolf, but to me he was more like a tiger. Every move he made was a smoldering combination of intimidating and enticing.

His lips curved up, he knew exactly what he was capable of. I squeezed my eyes shut, pushing together the tiny threads of my mind that hadn't come completely unglued.

"Allison," Deaghlan said. His smug expression confirmed that, yes, he absolutely knew the effect he had on me.

My face screwed up into what I hoped passed as a pleasant smile. I drew my knees up under my chin and wrapped my arms around my legs. Tearing my eyes from Deaghlan wasn't easy, but I managed to somehow focus on Ethan lying on the bed.

Deaghlan stood in front of me, and with one last smirk, he leaned over the bed and placed a hand on Ethan's forehead. He closed his eyes and bowed his head, not making a sound.

After several minutes, he opened his eyes and stood. I glanced over at Aodhan, still standing by the door. His face was completely blank, but I didn't miss the way his jaw stood out or that his knuckles were completely white.

"He's done," Deaghlan said, clasping his hands in front of his waist.

I looked down at the white tips of my sneakers. "Thanks."

I heard the sound of footsteps as Liam walked into the room. We all watched quietly as he paced for a moment.

"Liam, what is it?" I asked, unable to keep quiet for long.

He stopped pacing and leaned against the wall. He met my eyes briefly before rubbing his hands over his face.

"Your mother is adamant about not going home. But we don't have the amulet yet…we can't break the geis."

"Not going home?" I said. The rest I had already had

to accept.

"She's panicking about going back to the way she was. I can't even talk to her."

I dropped my feet to the floor and stood, not even looking in Deaghlan's direction. "Where is she?"

"In the gardens," Liam said. "But Allison, once we get her home safely, I'll figure out how to break the geis. I will. This will all be over soon."

Something cold trickled down my spinal cord. "To break the geis," I said, "we need Aoife's amulet, don't we?"

Liam shifted. "Well, yes."

"And where is Aoife?" I looked over at Deaghlan.

I hadn't said anything about the incident with Aoife to anyone, but Deaghlan and Saoirse must have known she'd somehow escaped the fey sphere.

"You make things so much more interesting, Allison," Deaghlan said. He arched his brow, a slow smile spreading across his features.

"Aoife will be dealt with," Saoirse said from the door. "But, now it's time for all of you to go home."

"I'll talk to my mom," I said, and I slid out the door, happy to let Saoirse and Deaghlan handle the rest of that conversation.

My mother sat alone on a stone bench in one of the many thriving gardens. This one was filled with what smelled like herbs.

Her head hung limp as she stared at her hands folded

in her lap. She lifted her chin as she heard me approach, though, and a hint of the mother I was used to stared back into my eyes. Not the Elizabeth from the stories my grandparents told, but the despondent mother I'd known most of my life.

I knew better than to be angry with her. None of this was her fault, I was well aware of that, but something snapped inside of me as I looked at her. Years of frustration and guilt bubbled up in my chest, bursting out in my words.

"You can't stay here," I said.

My mother nodded, looking back down at her hands. Her silence fueled my growing anger. Where was the strong, independent woman I'd heard so much about over the years? The rational part of my brain was appalled that I could feel this way, but the irrational side was much stronger at the moment.

"Do you remember my first day of kindergarten?" I said.

Her eyes jerked in my direction. "Yes," she said. "I was still lucid back then. Sometimes, anyway."

"I didn't want to go. I wanted to stay home with you and Gram. Do you remember what you said to me?"

My mother pressed her lips together and for a second I didn't think she'd answer me.

"No, not exactly. I just remember telling you that you had to go to school."

"You told me that you'd be right there waiting for me when I got off the bus. That's what got me through the day, knowing you'd still be there when I got home.

"No matter what happens Mom, I will be with you."

She took a deep breath and stood, looking at me with

bright green eyes. I held my hand out and together we walked back inside.

Chapter Fourteen

I tapped the steering wheel in time with a love song on the radio as I pulled into my grandparents' driveway. The song itself was upbeat, but the message was that two people in love were lost without each other.

I shifted into park and climbed out into the oppressive mid-August heat, my thighs sticking to the seat. This was the kind of heat that kept my grandparents in the house all day, especially since Pop had started having the discomfort in his chest. I hadn't had a choice, though—the graduate program I would be starting in the fall was holding orientation, and I couldn't miss it. I reached across the seat to grab my backpack, the words to the song still echoing in my ears.

The sound of Ethan's laughter came through my open window from Nicole's pool area, causing my heart to hiccup in my chest. I stood, grabbing the top corner of the door, trying to ignore that sound I loved so much. I hadn't seen him in the week we'd been back from Tír na n'Óg as we'd both been laid up with "mono." I'd only convinced

Gram I was feeling better two days ago.

I shut the car door and looked over at the fence surrounding the pool area. In a split second, I made a decision. I was tired of lying to myself and to everyone else. It had been a mistake to tell Ethan I didn't want him. That much was clear after everything that happened in Tír na n'Óg. I couldn't even remember a time in my life when I didn't want him.

The thought of him not giving me that stomach-tightening grin every time I saw him made my chest feel like a black hole. I couldn't be his friend, not now that I knew what it was like to be more.

I couldn't get to the gate fast enough. I fumbled with the latch, and it creaked as it swung open. I felt a ridiculous grin spreading on my face as I imagined telling Ethan how I really felt.

Nicole stood on the diving board, waiting to see who was coming in. Jeff was holding himself up with his arms resting over the side of the pool, and Ethan sat with his legs in the water of the shallow end. He was still laughing at something a petite blonde said as she stood gazing up at him from the water between his legs.

Dizziness flooded over me, as if all the air had been stolen from my lungs, and I froze as her hands moved suggestively up his thighs. When he turned my way, his smile fell, and for just a second we stared at each other.

"Hey, guys," I said, looking at Nicole and Jeff. "I just wanted to...let you know that I'm back from orientation." I tried to back away but stumbled, and my elbow hit the gate in a way that jarred my entire body.

Tears burned behind my eyes as I spun on my heel,

and let the gate swing closed behind me. I wanted to get out of there as fast as I could but skidded to a halt when I saw the three familiar men standing by my SUV. Liam, Aodhan, and Deaghlan watched as I made my walk of shame back from my cousin's house.

"Liam?" My mind registered that they must be waiting for me. Immediately my thoughts went to my mother. She should be in the house; I hadn't heard anything otherwise from Gram. "What's wrong?"

I vaguely heard the groaning of the gate opening behind me, and a voice calling out to me, but I was caught in Deaghlan's blue stare again, and he was pulling me toward him like a tractor beam.

"Al?"

The trance was broken when I realized it was Ethan saying my name.

I turned and saw him walking toward me, raking both of his hands through his damp hair.

I couldn't trust myself to speak, so I turned back to Liam, avoiding Deaghlan completely.

"Hello, Allison," Deaghlan said anyway as he sauntered over and kissed my forehead. As he pulled back, he stared hard at Ethan.

I peered back over my shoulder to see Ethan's eyes widen with surprise. He quickly looked over at Liam, his gaze questioning.

"What's going on?" I asked. "Why are you here?"

Liam cleared his throat, looking down at the ground. When he raised his eyes up to mine, his face was ashen.

"Aoife has escaped."

LAURA HOWARD

Pronunciation Guide

Liam{Lee-um}

Niamh{Neev}

Aoife{Ay-fuh}

Breanh{Bran}

Diarmuid{Der-mott}

Niall {Neal}

Blaithin{Blaw-heen}

Tagdh{Tag}

Eithne{En-ya}

Aodhan {Ay-den}

Saoirse{Sare-shuh}

Deaghlan{Deck-lun}

LAURA HOWARD

Acknowledgments

I may be the author of *The Forgotten Ones*, but I could never have done it alone.

I would like to thank editing goddess, Rebecca T Dickson, for spending hour after hour in the trenches with me, pushing me to Just Write!

My developmental editor, Danielle Poiesz, for helping me see through the chunk of stone that was draft one to the novel I present to the world.

My conceptual editor, Erin Reel, for spending time talking with me about my beloved characters and learning who they really were.

Diane J Reed for inspiring me to dig deeper into my soul.

Joanna Penn and Marie Forleo for teaching me that I could be creative and business savvy.

Autumn from Autumn Review, Andrea from The Bookish Babes, and Taryn Celucci from My Secret Romance for helping me understand the right way to approach Book Bloggers.

My amazing team of Super Sekrit Ninjas Peggy, Amy, Anna, Tobi and the entire gang for having faith in me before reading a word I wrote, and sharing my story with the world.

My Indie Girls for giving me a shoulder to cry on when I wasn't feeling like I could make it: Allie Brennan,

Nikki Jefford, Liz Long, Suzan Tisdale, Raine Thomas, Bethany Lopez and many more.

A special thanks to my husband and four incredible kids for not giving up on me when I've basically been AWOL this past year.

And lastly to my Mom and Dad for instilling in me that I could do anything if I believed in myself and didn't give up.

About the Author

Laura Howard lives in New Hampshire with her husband and four children. Her obsession with books began at the age of six when she got her first library card. *Nancy Drew*, *Sweet Valley High* and other girly novels were routinely devoured in single sittings. Books took a backseat to diapers when she had her first child. It wasn't until the release of a little novel called *Twilight*, eight years later, that she rediscovered her love of fiction. Soon after, her own characters began to make themselves known. *The Forgotten Ones* is her first published novel

For more information about author Laura Howard and her books, visit:

Blog:
http://laurahoward78.blogspot.com/

Twitter:
https://twitter.com/LauraHoward78

Facebook:
https://www.facebook.com/LauraHoward78

Enter your email address to receive updates on Laura Howard's work:
http://eepurl.com/yKniX.

191